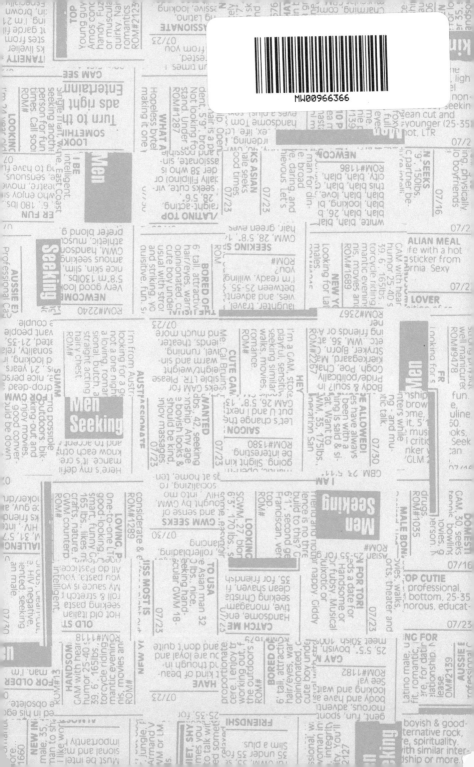

man of my DREAMS

man of my DREAMS

Provocative Writing on Men Loving Men

Edited by
Christopher Navratil

Introduction by
David Plante

CHRONICLE BOOKS
SAN FRANCISCO

Book & cover design by Cabra Diseño, Tin-tin Blackwell
Cover photograph by H. Freter.

Printed in Hong Kong.

Library of Congress Cataloging-in-Publication Data:
Man of my dreams :
    provocative writing on men loving men /
    edited by Christopher Navratil :
    introduction by David Plante.
    p.   cm.

ISBN 0-8118-1396-7
    1. Gay men—United States—Literary collections.
    2. Gay men—Sexual behavior—Literary collections.
    3. Gay men—United States—Biography.
    4. American literature—20th century.
    5. American literature—Men authors.
    6. Gay men's writings, American.
    7. Erotic stories, American.
    8. Love stories, American.
    I. Navratil, Christopher.
    PS509.H57M36 1996
    810.8'09206642—dc20   96-26172
                                                            CIP

Distributed in Canada by Raincoast Books
8680 Cambie Street
Vancouver, B.C. V6P 6M9

10 9 8 7 6 5 4 3 2 1

Chronicle Books
275 Fifth Street
San Francisco, CA 94103

Web Site: www.chronbooks.com

FOR THEIR ENCOURAGEMENT
AND ASSISTANCE I WOULD LIKE TO THANK
JAY SCHAEFER, BARBARA GORMAN,
JIM VAN BUSKIRK, PAMELA GEISMAR,
STEVE ANDERSON, AND MOST
ESPECIALLY KATE CHYNOWETH, WHOSE
PATIENCE, INSIGHT, AND SUPPORT
WERE INVALUABLE CONTRIBUTIONS
TO THIS PROJECT.

CONTENTS

PREFACE

Christopher Navratil

For me, becoming deeply involved in a relationship with another man can be as complicated as the solving of a mathematical equation. Compatibility, trust, intimacy, and (yikes) commitment are like the components in a complex formula, with the idea of a monogamous relationship equaling the sum of these parts. Never having been one to excel in math gives me, if nothing else, a reasonable excuse to sometimes steer clear of this challenge. Nonetheless, I continue to pursue men expecting that each new encounter will at least bring about something interesting if not always of lasting duration. I would like to believe that my intimate experiences are somehow unique. The men I spend significant time with, the men I spend brief time with, the beginnings, the endings, their roommates and family members, and occasionally even their pets (I once let a dead-end relationship linger for weeks until I realized that part of my attraction to the man was the fact that he had such an entertaining dog. Don't ask . . .) all make a lasting impression, whether we complete an equation or leave it dangling, unsolved.

Man of My Dreams collects fiction, poetry, drama, essays, and memoirs about men who are attracted to other men. Selections delve into the ordinary and the unusual moments in the pursuit of a relationship or, in some cases, the pursuit of just *a man*. The book is divided into six chapters, each focusing on a particular form or stage of attraction; they include hidden desires, first meetings, brief encounters, dealing with family and friends, breakup, and courtship. Many of the pieces in this collection might strike a familiar chord. The situations remind us that our own experiences, no matter how special or complex we might like to think them, are not all that uncommon. After all, there are only so many plot scenarios available, in life as well as in art.

The opening chapter, "Hidden Desires," exposes situations where sexual attraction, undermined by guilt or a fear of the unknown, remains submerged in secrecy. Many of the pieces in this section deal with adolescent desires. It's often thought the experimenting that goes on between teenage boys is just a phase in their sexual development, that once a boy grows into manhood his interests will turn to the opposite sex. The experiences related here, for the most part, disprove this notion and reveal deep emotional longings unlikely to ever be completely forgotten.

"First Meetings" takes a broad look at what can evolve from a significant introduction. The experiences range from the titillating moment of "The First Kiss" to the early seeds of obsession revealed in *The Folding Star*. The humor found in many of these passages should not come as a surprise—the anticipation that comes with a first meeting can create such inflated expectations that the risks of disappointment, or least disillusionment, are boundless. In the hands of a skilled humorist the opportunity to exploit this potentially awkward situation can be irresistible. Evelyn Waugh, Tennessee Williams, and Stephen McCauley take some delightful stabs at this subject.

Relationships seldom exist in a vacuum. Outside forces are often instrumental in determining the direction that one will take. The pieces in "Family & Friends" focus on relationships in the context of parents and well-meaning friends, on how their influence can have a nurturing or, in some cases, a disruptive effect on the individuals involved. How do parents react when their son brings home a lover to meet them? Why are friends so uncomfortable when a new significant other enters the picture? When no one approves, how much does it really matter?

"Breakup" touches on relationships that have come to an end or that never got off the ground in the first place. From James Merrill's bittersweet reunion with a former lover in *A Different Person* to the stinging disappointment of an unexpected brush-off in Felice Picano's "The Heart Has Its Reasons," the pieces in this section offer an intense array of emotional dramas with a couple of hilarious exceptions by David Sedaris and Armistead Maupin.

"I'm not really looking for a lover, but I'd like to meet *someone*," a friend remarks to T.R.Witomski in "How to Cruise the Met." The pursuit of sex for sex's sake, i.e., cruising, is the subject of "Brief Encounters." For some men, cruising is a way to avoid dealing with intimate emotions. For others it's more recreational, like shopping or opera—and sometimes it can become an obsession. Various forms of pursuit are explored here with amusing anecdotes (and some valuable tips) provided along the way.

The last section focuses on gay men attempting to find meaningful relationships. The first few pieces explore the early phases of courtship, often a time of emotional ambivalence; whether passionate or troubled, this is a stage where it's too early to tell if these relationships are destined for failure or success. Later in the section are pieces that go beyond this stage to express the views of those more ready to commit. Conflicts are still evident in a few of these relationships, but they seem to be outweighed by stronger feelings of assurance and comfort.

In considering which pieces to include in this anthology it was important to me that each writer provide an unusual or even contradictory perspective on gay relationships. And it certainly didn't hurt if the writer had a sense of humor. For the purposes of this project I chose only brief excerpts by most of the writers. The exceptions were a few complete works that were inherently short and concise: poems, a one-act play, a short, short story. My intention was to focus on the individual experiences without the distraction of other elements developed in the complete works. I purposely arranged the pieces in each section so as to provide a breadth of experience and encourage the reader to move from one excerpt to the next without losing focus on the particular subject. If never quite providing the key to a perfect relationship, I at least hope the anthology offers some useful insights and creates an entertaining, thought-provoking portrait of men loving men.

INTRODUCTION

David Plante

When I was in my early twenties in the early sixties, I lived in Boston, and there found my way into what was just beginning to be called the gay world. I recall sitting around a coffee table with new friends—all gay friends—and listening to stories: how Joe had picked up, along the Charles River Esplanade, a real hunk with a pecker (hands held wide apart) that long; how Harry had met in a bar and gone home with a real beauty of a guy who had a pecker (hands held wider apart) that long; how Sean had been to the tubs and in the steam met a guy. . . . And I, who had no stories to tell, was roused into a state of anguish by my friends' stories—a state of being possessed by muscle-twisting sexual longing and soul-twisting sexual envy.

Even if I had been more sexually experienced than I was, I would, I think, have felt the same because I would have had only my friends' stories with which to compare my experiences, and I wasn't sure if these stories were fantasy or not. I kept entirely to myself that the stories had no real relevance to my limited experience, to my fear of even walking alone along the Esplanade, to my spending hours and hours in a bar trying to make contact and never going home with the guy I most wanted to but someone I convinced myself was as beautiful as I could ever have, to my most often going home on my own.

Not that I ever let any of my friends suspect that my sexual life was any less enviable than theirs. I learned to elaborate my stories to make my friends as envious of me as I was of them. What I made of the German who modelled swimsuits! But this only added to my anguish, because elaborating stories to make my friends as envious of me as I was of them left me feeling sick with unrealized and, I thought, unrealizable longing.

None of the fiction about gay sex and love of the time was any real help. The most important of these was James Baldwin's *Giovanni's Room*, and though it set a precedent for taking sex between men as a fact that needed no justification, there was something unconvincing about it, for it seemed to have more to do with wish fulfillment than reality. At the time, homosexuality itself seemed to be based on wish fulfillment.

Whenever, then, I tried to write stories about my experiences, I always found that sexual fantasy was stronger than my determination to be factual. It was as if I were making myself envious of my sexual fantasy, which flowered in my prose like huge artificial roses from the centers of which emerged the heads and naked shoulders and chests and groins and erect cocks of beautiful young men. I was indulging myself, and I had to throw these stories out.

An anthology such as *Man of My Dreams* would have made all the difference to me. It is a very funny anthology, and it might have taught me a degree of irony and humor, which I, in my intense seriousness, needed; it might also have taught me how to describe tender intimacies without embarrassment; but above all, in it I would have read stories—though mostly excerpts of longer works, the pieces chosen by Christopher Navratil are self-contained, highly suggestive stories—that had everything to do with my sexual life as I lived it, and it would have taught me a way of writing about sexual life that was quite as factual as it was fabulous.

Take a story like Daniel Curzon's "Two Bartenders, a Butcher and Me," which is about perhaps the most fabulous of homosexual fantasies, an orgy, but this story of an orgy in a motel room with a big tray of dirty dishes and half-eaten food on one of the double beds is written from the point of view of a participant who is worried about his small dick. I can easily imagine a close version of this story in a porn magazine, because it is as vividly graphic in its depiction of sex as porn, but it is also, in the very directness of its style, a totally convincing account of the experience of four guys trying to realize fantasy as fact. The story doesn't deny fantasy sex but uses it very much to the advantage of its account of real life sex, and the story charms.

That most of the work included in this anthology has been published within the last fifteen years is altogether telling. (Of the older writers, Lytton Strachey's letter was a private joke, Evelyn Waugh's portrayal of Sebastian Flyte with his teddy bear keeps sex out of it, and Tennessee Williams's poem keeps his characters burnt up in bed in a hotel fire sexually anonymous; Joe Orton's explicit diaries were published only in 1986.) *Man of My Dreams* shows that there is growing, more and more powerfully and self-confidently, a muscular body of writing about gay sex and love and life that exposes the pimples on the back, the hair around the nipples, the hernia scar, but that remains very attractive, very sexy.

And what *Man of My Dreams* also shows is that that body is seen in as many different ways as there are writers considering gay experiences carefully and writing about them in their own entirely individual styles. Even these fragments of writing embody the total individuality of the writers; for example, the excerpt from Alan Hollinghurst's *The Folding Star* reveals all the evocative richness of his novels, and the excerpt from Francis King's *Secret Lives* the evocative simplicity of his. The writers represented here are, in terms of their very styles, in control of their material, and they use their material to express their altogether individual views. Nothing breaks down stereotypes as effectively. And it is in the very individuality of each gay experience that one finds what is most common to the writers in *Man of My Dreams*—they are aware, even when they are being as camp as the campiest fag, that gay sex and love and life are real sex and real love and real life, because the sex and love and life of each gay man is the sex and love and life of an individual in the world.

And what is most heartening about this anthology is that *because* the characters are in the real world of individual lives—difficult families and complicated straight friends and (imagine!) baseball teams with ball-breaking coaches; disillusionments and infidelities and black eyes; and above all, terrifying sickness and death due to AIDS—these gay men can say that they love one another without their love sounding in any way like fantasy, but as a wonderful fact. Setting such examples is what writing is so much about.

Hidden DeSireS

A HOME AT THE END
OF THE WORLD

Michael Cunningham

APRIL CAME. IT WAS NOT SWIMMING WEATHER YET, BUT I INSISTED that we go to the quarry as soon as the last scabs of old snow had disappeared from the shadows. I knew we'd go swimming naked. I was rushing the season.

It was one of those spring days that emerge scoured from the long, long freeze, with a sky clear as melted snow. The first hardy, thick-stemmed flowers had poked out of the ground. The quarry, which lay three miles out of town, reflected sky on a surface dark and unmoving as obsidian. Except for a long caramel-colored cow that had wandered down from a pasture to drink in the shallows, Bobby and I were the only living things there. We might have hiked to a glaciated lake high in the Himalayas.

"Beautiful," he said. We were passing a joint. A blue jay rose, with a single questioning shrill, from an ash tree still in bud.

"We have to swim," I said. "We have to."

"Still too cold," he said. "That water'd be freezing, man."

"We have to, anyway. Come on. It's the first official swim of summer. If we don't swim today, it'll start snowing again tomorrow."

"Who told you that?"

"Everybody knows it. Come *on.*"

"Maybe," he said. "Awful cold, though."

By then we had reached the gravel bed that passed for a beach, where the cow, who stood primly at the water's edge, stared at us with coal-black eyes. This quarry had a rough horseshoe shape, with limestone cliffs that rose in a jagged half circle and then fell back again to the beach.

"It's not the least bit cold," I said to Bobby. "It's like Bermuda by this time of year. Watch me."

Spurred by my fear that we would do no more that day than smoke a joint, fully clothed, beside a circle of dark water, I started up the shale-strewn slope that led to the clifftop. The nearer cliffs were less than twenty feet high, and in summer the more courageous swimmers dove from there into the deep water. I had never even thought of diving off the cliff before. I was nothing like brave. But that day I scrambled in my cowboy boots, which still pinched, up the slope to the cracked limestone platform that sprouted, here and there, a lurid yellow crocus.

"It's summer up here," I shouted back to Bobby, who stood alone on the beach, cupping the joint. "Come on," I shouted. "Don't test the water with your fingers, just come up here and we'll dive in. We've got to."

"Naw, Jon," he called. "Come back."

With that, I began taking off my clothes in a state of humming, high-blown exhilaration. This was a more confident, daring Jonathan standing high on a sun-warmed rock, stripping naked before the puzzled gaze of a drinking cow.

"Jon," Bobby called, more urgently.

As I pulled off my shirt and then my boots and socks, I knew a raw abandon I had never felt before. The sensation grew as each new patch of skin touched the light and the cool, brilliant air. I could feel myself growing lighter, taking on possibility, with every stitch I removed. I got ungracefully out of my jeans and boxer shorts, and stood for a moment, scrawny, naked, and wild, touched by the cold sun.

"This is it," I hollered.

Bobby, far below, said, "Hey, man, no—"

And for the sake of Bobby, for the sake of my new life, I dove.

A thin sheet of ice still floated on the water, no more than a membrane, invisible until I broke through it. I heard the small crackling, felt the ice splinter around me, and then I was plunged into unthinkable cold, a cold that stopped my breath and seemed, for a long moment, to have stopped my heart as well. My flesh itself shrank, clung in animal panic to the bone, and I thought with perfect clarity, I'm dead. This is what it's like.

Then I was on the surface, breaking through the ice a second time. My consciousness actually slipped out of my body, floated up, and in retrospect I have a distinct impression of watching myself swim to shore, gasping, lungs clenched like fists, the ice splintering with every stroke, sending diamond slivers up into the air.

Bobby waded in to his thighs to help pull me out. I remember the sight of his wet jeans, clinging darkly to his legs. I remember thinking his boots would be ruined.

It took another moment for my head to clear sufficiently to realize he was screaming at me, even as he helped me out of the water.

"Goddamn it," he yelled, and his mouth was very close to my ear. "Oh, goddamn you. God*damn*."

I was too concerned with my own breathing to respond. He got us well up onto the gravel before letting go of me and launching into a full-scale rant. The best I could do was stand, breathing and shivering, as he shouted.

At first he strode back and forth in a rigid pattern, as if touching two invisible goals ten feet apart, screaming "You motherfucker, you stupid motherfucker." As he shouted, his circuit between the two goals grew shorter and shorter, until he was striding in tight little circles, following the pattern of a coiled spring. His face was magenta. Finally he stopped walking, but still he turned completely around, three times, as if the spring were continuing to coil inside him. All the while he screamed. He stopped calling me a motherfucker and began making sounds I could not understand, a stream of infuriated babble that seemed directed not at me but at the sky and the cliffs, the mute trees.

I watched dumbly. I had never seen wrath like that before; I had not known it occurred in everyday life. There was nothing for me to do but wait, and hope it ended.

After some time, without saying what he was going to do, Bobby ran off to retrieve my clothes from the clifftop. Though his fury had quieted somewhat, it was by no means spent. I stood nude on the gravel, waiting for him. When he came back with my clothes and boots he dumped them in a pile at my feet, saying, "Put 'em on fast," in a tone of deep reproach. I did as I was told.

When I had dressed he draped his jacket around me, over my own. "No, you need it," I said. "Your pants are all wet . . ."

"Shut up," he told me, and I did.

We started back to the highway, where we would hitch a ride to town. On the way Bobby put his arm around my shoulders and held me close to him. "Stupid fucker," he muttered. "Stupid, stupid. *Stu*pid." He continued holding me as we stood with our thumbs out by the roadside, and continued holding me in the back of the Volkswagen driven by the two Oberlin students who picked us up. He kept his arm around me all the way home, muttering.

Back at my house, he ran a scalding-hot shower. He all but undressed me, and ordered me in. Only after I was finished, and wrapped in towels, did he take off his own wet clothes and get in the shower himself. His bare skin was bright pink in the steamy bathroom. When he emerged, glistening, studded with droplets, the medallion of pale hair was plastered to his chest.

We went to my room, put on Jimi Hendrix, and rolled a joint. We sat in our towels, smoking. "Stupid," he whispered. "You could have killed yourself. You know how I'd have felt if you'd done that?"

"No," I said.

"I'd have felt like, I don't know."

And then he looked at me with such sorrow. I put the joint down in the ashtray and, in an act of courage that far outstripped jumping off a cliff into icy water—that exceeded all my brave acts put together—I reached out and laid my hand on his forearm. There it was, his arm, sinewy and golden-haired, under my fingers. I looked at the floor—the braided rug and pumpkin-colored planks. Bobby did not pull his arm away.

A minute passed. Either nothing or something had to happen. In terror, with my pulse jumping at my neck, I began to stroke his arm with the tip of my index finger. Now, I thought, he will see what I'm after. Now he'll bolt in horror and disgust. Still I kept on with that single miniature gesture, in a state of fear so potent it was indistinguishable from desire. He did not recoil, nor did he respond.

Finally I managed to look at his face. His eyes were bright and unblinking as an animal's, his mouth slack. I could tell he was frightened too, and it was his fear that enabled me to move my hand to his bare shoulder. His skin prickled with gooseflesh over the smooth broad curve of his scapula. I could feel the subtle rise and fall of his breathing.

Quickly, because I lacked the nerve for deliberation, I moved my hand to his thigh. He twitched and grimaced, but did not retreat. I burrowed my hand in under the towel he wore. I watched expressions of fear and pleasure skate across his eyes. Because I had no idea what to do, I replicated the strokes I'd used on myself. When he stiffened in my hand it seemed like a gesture of forgiveness.

Then he put out a hand and, with surprising delicacy, touched me, too. We did not kiss. We did not embrace. Jimi sang "Purple Haze." The furnace rumbled from deep in the house. Steam hissed through the pipes.

We mopped up with Kleenexes afterward, and dressed in silence. Once we were dressed, however, Bobby relit the joint and began talking in his usual voice about usual things: the Dead's next concert tour, our plan to get jobs and buy a car together. We passed the joint and sat on the floor of my room like any two American teenagers, in an ordinary house surrounded by the boredom and struggling green of an Ohio spring. Here was another lesson in my continuing education: like other illegal practices, love between boys was best treated as commonplace. Courtesy demanded that one's fumbling, awkward performance be no occasion for remark, as if in fact one had acted with the calm expertise of a born criminal.

[1990]

SCISSORS, PAPER, ROCK

Fenton Johnson

THEY STOP FOR THE NIGHT AT WIGWAM VILLAGE, A BUNGALOW MOTEL outside Emporia, Kansas. The bungalows are built to resemble tepees, reinforced concrete over a tent of rusting I-beams. They range in a circle around a cracked and rusting swimming pool. The pop and click of a red neon sign (OTEL—OTEL—OTEL) is the only wound.

Willy emerges from the office, holding a key high. "We are in number nine," he says, and sets about scanning numbers over tepee doors.

The motel manager—big-busted, black-haired with pink curlers—props herself against the office doorjamb, holding a shoulder bag. "Kind of young to be traveling alone," she says to Raphael.

"I'm almost nineteen years old," Raphael says. "And I'm not alone."

She saunters to Raphael's side, runs a frank hand over his chest. Some visceral part of him grumbles and contracts. He stuffs his hands into the back pockets of his jeans and scuffs a toe at the rich Kansas loam, so different from the thin, stony soil of the Kentucky hills. "Relatives don't count," she says.

"Relatives?"

"Your brother."

"There must be some mistake," Raphael says. "He's not my brother."

The manager's eyes drift shut, then she opens them and steps back. "Figures. You run a motel, you see it all." She drops the bag. "Whatever he is, he left his purse." Raphael retrieves it from the dust.

"A picture!" Willy beckons from the wigwam door, waving an Instamatic. "We must have a picture. You must ask the manager if she will take it."

"No pictures with me. No way."

Willy points to the wigwams. "But this is America."

"*Your* America, maybe. Not mine." Raphael takes his shaving kit from the car and enters the room, dodging the camera in Willy's outstretched hand.

Number nine has only one bed, a small double. At the sight Raphael's gut ties itself in a small, terrified fist, but he quells his fears. After all, he is the driver, the native son, the English speaker. He is cool; he is in control. "I have a girlfriend," he says with studied casualness. "I'm meeting her in San Francisco."

"Of course," Willy says, tucking the camera in his bag. "You are an American, child of the seventies. You will meet your girlfriend in California, where you will marry by the ocean and go to the university in law." Willy laughs and squeezes Raphael's shoulder. "Or business." He ruffles Raphael's hair, then stretches his hands over his head, popping his knuckles and yawning.

"I have to be in California in three days," Raphael says. "I'm meeting my girlfriend in San Francisco on Thursday. I'm not stopping except to sleep." He takes a deep breath, then delivers the punch. "Maybe I should take you to some likely-looking place and let you out. You could get a ride with somebody who's taking his time to see the country."

Willy cocks his head. "Your car is not healthy?"

"My car is just fine."

"You are in luck. I am a mechanic." Willy pulls a film can and a pipe from his shoulder bag. "You want to get high?"

Raphael hesitates. He has never smoked marijuana. To accept this hospitality is to choose to allow Willy to continue on. He thinks of the temperature gauge on the Rambler, which for most of the day hovered near boiling. He studies the pipe, which Willy has thrust into his hand.

The pipe is small, hand-molded from some jade-green clay. It fits comfortably in his palm, a compact, tangible correlation of the vast, extraordinary, unimagined experiences that await him, of the gap between the whitewashed world that has penetrated to the remote hills and hollows of his childhood, and the vast, astounding, seductive, inviting world as it really is. He takes the pipe to his lips. In this gesture, in this moment his world divides and complicates itself, a geometrically progressing mitosis whose end he cannot foresee or imagine.

"That woman, with the pink things in her hair," Willy says. "She insulted my accent. I have no accent."

Raphael demurs tactfully—he is a Southern boy, he knows his manners. "Just a *little* accent."

"A *bitch*," Willy says, with feeling.

For the first time in his life Raphael finds himself siding with the curler-headed motel managers and greasy-spoon owners of the hinterlands. "A Kansan," he says. "An American. A *true* American. What do you expect?"

"Cowboys," Willy says. "At least, that is what I am looking for. But we are not yet far enough west."

Willy strips and climbs into bed. Watching from the corner of his eye, Raphael sees that he wears small, tight underwear, striped in some pattern of green and navy blue. Raphael's groin tightens. Resolutely he turns his eyes to the wall and steps out of his jeans, but his eyes have taken on a life of their own—they know what they want, and it is stronger than what his mind wants, and he cannot keep himself from turning and looking. He retreats to the bathroom, where he shuts and locks the door.

Lingering over his toothbrush, he considers those parts of his life that until a few weeks before he assumed no one in the world shared. Then he went for his induction physical, to encounter its questionnaire's forthright acknowledgment (*homosexual tendencies?*) of the slow, swelling, sub-cutaneous movements that until then he had allowed himself to acknowl-edge only in secret, and then only long enough to deny that they exist.

Why has he encouraged Willy's talk of free morals, free love, free sex? Why did he pick up this strange red-haired man in the first place? Why has he allowed Willy to stay? Raphael leans his head against the mirror, staring down his reflection.

Leaving the bathroom, he crawls under the covers, still wearing his underwear, his T-shirt, his socks. He is settling himself when Willy flings an arm over his shoulder, carelessly, as if Raphael's back were the most convenient armrest.

The mattress sags, hopelessly. Raphael clings to its edge to keep from sliding downhill into the hollow created by Willy's weight. He lies on his stomach, crushing his arms to pins and needles, until long after Willy's feigned snores have given way to shallow breathing.

His nails dug into the mattress, Willy's hand dangling before his eyes, Raphael falls into a place between waking and sleep. Behind his eyelids the road unrolls endlessly. At his side sits a California woman, blonde and tanned—but Raphael turns, and it is red-headed Willy, in a Stetson hat and a pearl-buttoned shirt.

Raphael wakes. Overhead, nesting in the wigwam peak, sparrows chatter. The paper blinds blink: gray with dawn; lurid with neon light. In his half-sleep he has turned over, slid down into the bed's hollow. Willy's hand is working its way under the elastic of his underwear, his fingers lingering in the curl of Raphael's pubic hair.

Raphael lies stiff, frozen, clammy with sweat. He tells himself that this is not happening, that he is not here, that he wants only to be in California, where he will find what he is looking for. He wants only this: to get where he is going. At almost nineteen years old, is this so much to ask?

At the thought he rises abruptly. Willy's hand flops against the bed-clothes. Raphael heads for the shower, where he stays until he is certain the hot water has run out, and that Willy's shower will be cold.

[1993]

THE LIAR

Stephen Fry

IT HAD BEEN UPSTAIRS, IN THE LONG DORM. THE ROOM WAS EMPTY, the floorboards squeaking more faintly than usual beneath his tread. Cartwright's cubicle had its curtain drawn. The distant moan of whistles and cheers on the Upper Games Field and the nearer bang of a downstairs door slamming shut had unsettled him. They were over-familiar, with a bogus, echoing quality, a staginess that put him on his guard. The whole school knew he was here. They knew he liked to creep about the House alone. They were watching, he was convinced of it. The background shouts of rugger and hockey weren't real, they were part of a taped sound-track played to deceive him. He was walking into a trap. It had always been a trap. No one had ever believed in him. They signed him off games and let him think that he had the House to himself. But they knew, they had always known. Tom, Bullock, Heydon-Bayley, even Cartwright. Especially Cartwright. They watched and they waited. They all knew and they all bided their time until the moment they had chosen for his exposure and disgrace.

Let them watch, let them know. Here was Cartwright's bed and under the pillow, here, yes, here the pyjamas. Soft brushed cotton, like Cart-wright's soft brushed hair and a smell, a smell that was Cartwright to the last molecule. There was even a single gold hair shining on the collar, and there, just down there, a new aroma, an aroma, an essence that rippled outwards from the centre of the whole Cartwrightness of Cartwright.

For Adrian other people did not exist except as extras, as bit-players in the film of his life. No one but he had noted the splendour and agony of existence, no one else was truly or fully alive. He alone gasped at dew trapped in cobwebs, at spring buds squeaking into life. Afternoon light bouncing like a yo-yo in a stream of spittle dropping from a cow's lips, the slum-wallpaper peel of bark on birches, the mash of wet leaves pulped into pavements, they grew and burst only in him. Only he knew what it was to love.

Haaaaaaah . . . if they really were watching then now was the time to pull back the curtain and jeer, now was the time to howl contempt.

But nothing. No yells, no sneers, no sound at all to burst the swollen calm of the afternoon.

Adrian trembled as he stood and did himself up. It was an illusion. Of course it was an illusion. No one watched, no one judged, no one pointed or whispered. Who were they, after all? Low-browed, scarlet-naped rugger-buggers with no more grace and vision than a jockstrap.

Sighing, he had moved to his own cubicle and laid out the astrakhan coat and top hat.

If you can't join them, he thought, beat them.

He had fallen in love with Hugo Alexander Timothy Cartwright the moment he laid eyes on him, when, as a string of five new arrivals, the boy had trickled into evening hall the first night of Adrian's second year.

Heydon-Bayley nudged him.

"What do you reckon, Healey? Lush, or what?"

For once Adrian had remained silent. Something was terribly wrong.

It had taken him two painful terms to identify the symptoms. He looked them up in all the major textbooks. There was no doubt about it. All the authorities concurred: Shakespeare, Tennyson, Ovid, Keats, Georgette Heyer, Milton, they were of one opinion. It was love. The Big One.

Cartwright of the sapphire eyes and golden hair, Cartwright of the Limbs and Lips: He was Petrarch's Laura, Milton's Lycidas, Catullus's Lesbia, Tennyson's Hallam, Shakespeare's fair boy and dark lady, the moon's Endymion. Cartwright was Garbo's salary, the National Gallery, he was cellophane: he was the tender trap, the blank unholy surprise of it all and the bright golden haze on the meadow: he was honey-honey, sugar-sugar, chirpy chirpy cheep-cheep and his baby-love: the voice of the turtle could be heard in the land, there were angels dining at the Ritz and a nightingale sang in Berkeley Square.

Adrian had managed to coax Cartwright into an amusing half-hour in the House lavs two terms previously, but he had never doubted he could get the trousers down: that wasn't it. He wanted something more from him than the few spasms of pleasure that the limited activities of rubbing and licking and heaving and pushing could offer.

He wasn't sure what the thing was that he yearned for, but one thing he did know. It was less acceptable to love, to ache for eternal companionship, than it was to bounce and slurp and gasp behind the five courts. Love was Adrian's guilty secret, sex his public pride.

[1991]

INVISIBLE LIFE

E. Lynn Harris

BASIL'S BACKSIDE CAPTURED MY ATTENTION AS I WALKED THROUGH the huge lobby of the Hilton Hotel. He was bending over signing the T-shirt of a little boy who had recognized him. I walked up behind him and stood there as he held a conversation with the fan. When he noticed the little boy looking at me behind him, he turned to face me. We exchanged perfunctory handshakes and gave each other the once over.

"Ray." He smiled. "I'm glad you could make it. This is Joey."

"Hello, Joey. Are you a big football fan?"

"Yes sir, the biggest!" exclaimed the small redhead.

Basil spent a few more minutes talking with Joey and then suggested that we try the Oyster Bar for drinks and a quick bite. We both ordered Coronas with lime and took seats at a small table next to the window that faced the Avenue of the Americas.

"Nice suit, Mr. Tyler. Perry Ellis?"

"Yes, it is."

"You wear it very well. That tie is too sharp, man."

"Thanks a lot. So Basil, why the alias?" I asked.

"No particular reason. Is Kyle your friend's real name?"

"I think so. I've known him by that name for over six years. How did you two meet?"

"Didn't Kyle tell you?"

"No, he didn't."

"Well, let's just say it was a mutual friend."

"A mutual friend?"

"Yes, but I don't want to talk about Kyle. I want to talk about you."

"Me?"

"Yes, you know I'm surprised that Kyle has friends like you."

"Why do you say that?"

"Well, let's face it, Kyle's a flaming faggot."

"Say, man, you're talking about my best friend. I put the term *faggot* in the same category as *nigger*. Besides, what are you?" I felt my face redden from anger.

"Ray, I'm sorry. I *deal* sometimes, but I consider myself straight."

"Good for you. Then I don't think we have anything else to talk about."

I reached for my coat and briefcase when Basil stood up and said, "Raymond, I'm sorry. Please don't leave right now."

I slowly sat back down but held on to my coat and briefcase. Basil started to talk about how he had been introduced to the life by a rich alumnus while he was playing college football. He said he did it because he needed the money. "He gave me head. My girlfriend wouldn't."

"So the money made your dick hard?" I asked with a smirk.

"Come on, Ray, give me a break. Put yourself in my position."

"I can't do that," I replied coldly.

As he continued to talk, I noticed how really handsome Basil was. His honey-colored skin was clear and smooth and his eyes sparkled like polished silver bullets as he talked. Basil explained how hard it was going both ways and being in the public eye. He had to be careful whom he talked to about certain things, and eventually he would have to get married. He also said that there were several professional players, both football and basketball, who were *in*, but that it was the most secretive of cliques. He added that track-and-field guys were notorious for being *in*.

I pumped him for names I would recognize, but he politely declined to name names. As he talked, I realized that there were several things to like about Basil, but an equal number of reasons to dislike him.

He would use the word *faggot* as effortlessly as one sprinkled salt on hot buttered popcorn. Every time he used the word, I raised my eyebrows and he quickly apologized. I got the impression that it was part of his everyday vocabulary.

"So do you consider yourself bisexual?" I asked.

"No, not really."

"Gay?"

"Fuck no."

"Then what did you want to talk with me about?"

"Well, I like the way you look. I mean, you don't look gay." Basil paused and then said, "I was wondering if we could hook up the next time I'm in the city?"

"What does gay look like, Basil?"

"You know." He shrugged. "What about my question?"

"To talk about sports and stuff? Sure, I'm as big a football fan as your friend Joey."

"Is that all we could do?" he asked in an amorous tone.

"I think so. I'm seeing someone."

"Who is he?"

"Who said it was a he?"

I finished my beer and Basil gave me his phone number at three different places, including his mom's and his girlfriend's house. When he stood up I couldn't believe that I was turning Basil down as a potential suitor.

His body was a sculptor's vision. I smiled to myself at how easily 'I'm seeing someone' fell from my lips. Whom was I talking about, Quinn or Nicole?

"So you're still not going to tell me how you met Kyle?"

"No, I'd better not. If you and Kyle are as close as you say, then I'm surprised you don't know." We again traded handshakes and I wished him good luck on the upcoming football season and his desire for a complete heterosexual adjustment. He let out a hearty laugh and told me he would give me a call and invite me to a game next season. He walked with me out to the street so I could catch a taxi uptown.

"I'm going to meet Kyle. Should I tell him you say hello?"

"Sure, why not. Kyle's cool," Basil said.

"I'll tell him you said that."

As I rode uptown, I wondered what the big secret was about where Kyle and Basil had met. Kyle had a gift for meeting men anywhere he went and I knew most of his other friends. I knew men like Basil didn't frequent bars, but they cruised the subways and other public places. New York City was famous for its *tea rooms*, a term used for the restrooms in the subways. Kyle told me about all the married men he met there. He said that traffic had decreased since AIDS hit the city. Somehow I managed not to become involved in this seedy side of the life, which also included gay bathhouses. I tried hard not to pass judgment on Kyle and others who chose that route. I learned not to be surprised at the number of professional black men who led secret lives. Had I stayed in Alabama, my life would have become similar. There was no way I would involve my family in my gay lifestyle. Besides, I came to realize that it was a lifestyle and not my life.

In Alabama I would also have had to be concerned with fraternity brothers who lived in the city. Maybe this was one of the reasons I loved living in New York City. When you left your place of employment, your life became your own.

[1991]

THE SPELLING LESSON

Liam Brosnahan

"Suture: s-u-t-u-r-e, suture."

Father Kane and I were performing surgery on the yard behind the rectory. The pictures of bounteous trellises in the rectory parlor had inspired him. So Saturday found him—and me, always keen to please—combining spelling and seedlings under a blazing noonday sun.

"Scalpel," said Dan Kane, wiping sweat from the end of his chin on the dusty leg of his dungarees.

I chose a trowel from the rusted garden tools heaped before me and placed it in the young priest's hand. Five quick scoops dug a bowl in the ground just large enough to accommodate the root ball of a rosebush on which several green buds looked close to bloom.

"So, Champ..."

"Yes, Father?"

"How are things proceeding with Lucinda?"

"Proceeding?"

"Have you osculated her yet?"

"*Father?*"

Tamping the earth back into place around the roots, the sweat-shirted priest began to laugh.

"The word is 'osculate.'"

"But what does it mean?" I asked, dreading to know.

"Spell it first, then look it up."

Unlike the two nuns who had tutored me before, who fished their words from oceans of books, Dan Kane just snatched words as they rode by on trains of thought.

"Osculate: o-s-c-u-l-a-t-e, osculate?"

"You have a good ear, Champ. There's a Webster's on the shelf in the monsignor's study."

I gasped. The pastor's sanctum, to my knowledge, had never been breached by any parishioner, adult or child, currently alive. I paused at its murky threshold, waiting for my sun-blind eyes to adjust to the velvet-draped gloom. A dagger of sunlight cut across the rug and desk, pointing up the wall of shelves to the spine of the book I sought. Though I knew Monsignor Skinner was in Baltimore for the weekend, I tiptoed across the thick carpet.

Osculate, I read: *to kiss.*

"Very funny," I said aloud and returned the book to the shelf. My vision now adjusted to the dim surroundings, I took advantage of this rare chance to check out the room.

Outside the arched window, something clanged to the ground.

An ancient spade, still caked with the mud from the backyard, lay on the concrete near the spot where Kane was hopping and chanting, "Jesus, Mary, and Joseph," like dirty words.

A guilty chuckle stuck in my throat as my voice broke again, and my breath cut off in a gasp.

Violently shaking his dripping curls, Kane blessed the yard and my window with a spray of perspiration. Then, his back to the rectory, he lifted both arms and peeled off his sodden sweatshirt in one smooth movement.

My eyes, like telescopes, fixed on his back. As he knotted his fingers behind his head to stretch, streams of sweat converged into the trench of his spine from under wide curves of bulging muscle.

"Wings!" I gasped.

My own flesh shivered as a trickle of perspiration slid down my backbone like the tip of an icy finger. On the other side of the glass, the stretching continued.

His arms, like those of a child playing airplane, extended straight out from his torso, turning round and round in circles.

"Wings," I whispered again, but fainter, much fainter than before.

The "wings" dropped down to his sides then raised straight to heaven as, with a loud yawn, he appeared to climb an invisible rope. The muscles in his back clenched and knotted and smoothed again as he segued into touching his toes in sharp downward thrusts.

I didn't realize how long I'd been watching, or that I'd been counting his bends, until I heard myself say, "Fifty." My absence, I felt suddenly, must seem suspiciously long.

At that very moment, Father Kane turned in the direction of the window.

My jaw fell open at the sight of his chest. A dense lawn of dark hair spread across it, tapering like an inverted Christmas tree pointing at his zipper. Something seemed to lodge behind my Adam's apple that would not be swallowed away. My heart was pounding.

"Hey, Champ!"

With a bolt of panic, I jumped back from the window, but when my name was called again, I heard with relief only his eagerness to return to our task. I had not been seen.

At the kitchen door, I met him coming in, pulling on his sweatshirt.

"I got caught up in the dictionary," I said.

"Dictionaries are like hardware stores," he smiled. "After you get home with the six kinds of nails you found, you realize you forgot the hammer you went there to buy."

I tried to smile, but my mouth wouldn't cooperate.

"So, did you find what you were looking for?" he asked.

"Osc—Osculate, to kiss." My lungs weren't helping either, and I swallowed the word "kiss."

"No, I haven't."

"Haven't what, Champ?"

"Haven't osculated Lucinda." I looked away from him and glanced from wall to wall to floor, trying to avoid the sight of his face and, especially, his mouth. "I've never kissed anybody."

"No one?" he sounded amused and skeptical. "Not even your mother?"

I winced. "There's only my grandfather and my brother. I guess we're not the kissy type."

"Oh. I'm sorry, Cham—"

"I hate the name 'Champ,'" I suddenly barked, surprising myself. It wasn't even true.

"Then Franny it is," the priest said, somewhat taken aback. "You know, it's no disgrace to be thirteen and never-been-kissed—"

I wanted, all at once, I didn't know why, to hit somebody. Father Kane was a handy target, but, even more, at the moment, I felt like slugging myself.

"I don't care if it's a disgrace or not!" I cried. "In fact, I like it better if it is. I'm never going to kiss anybody, ever. Who needs a stupid kiss? I don't!"

My voice was zigzagging upward in pitch. I was aware that I was babbling, but, to my horror, I was unable to control my tongue.

"Franny," Kane said soothingly. "It's okay, it's all okay—"

My anger swerved abruptly to embarrassment and to fear I had hurt his feelings. I glanced up and my eyes locked on the curve of his lips, which were parted in confused helplessness before the adolescent genie he had unleashed but could not seem to command.

Unable to force my eyes from his face, I turned my back.

"Franny?"

"I'm sorry, Father," I said weakly. "I'm . . . I'm very thirsty," I said, which was true enough but came so unbidden to my lips that I was only half-sure I was the one who said it.

Kane leapt on it like a chance at sudden wealth. He guided me to a chair at the kitchen table and proceeded to pour us both some iced tea from the refrigerator, all the while blaming himself for working me too hard in the bright sun. "Just a little overwrought," he said nervously.

"Silent *w*, right?" I said, still avoiding his face.

"Excuse me?"

"There's a *w* in the middle of 'overwrought,' right?"

"Yeah," he chuckled, "I guess there is."

I managed to echo a credible chuckle and even returned the feeble smile he gave me. Was I up to more spelling stumpers, he asked. Sure, ha-ha, I answered, just try me, ha-ha.

Ha-ha-ha.

Ha-ha-ha.

Everything was fine again. I had merely been overwrought—nearly sunstroked. The sun could get you really confused. People in the desert died of too much sun.

"The word is 'irreversible.'"

I would be careful from now on to walk only in the shade.

"The word is 'awakening.'"

Things that were usually good for you could be dangerous if you overdid them.

"The word is 'mystagogy.'"

I was back in control. Letters were easier to speak than words.

The words were "hirsute," "avatar," "perspiration" and "serendipitous," "jeopardy," "precipice." Kane grinned another prize-winning smile. I looked away.

I had forgotten something. Something I was supposed to do here today.

"The word is 'proscribe.'"

"Excuse me, Father?"

"Daydreaming about Lucinda, eh? The word is 'proscribe.'"

"May I have the definition?"

Kane stood up. "Let's do this right. I'll go get the dictionary."

It was when he walked past my chair that the lightning struck.

Like the gentle breeze that harbingers a tornado, a light wind fluttered the curtains and spiraled round the priest before it found my nose. Molecules of fresh, salty sweat flew up my nostrils and exploded into atoms that raced to my brain like couriers on horseback proclaiming the meaning of life. I received the news in a scalp that shrank, in earlobes that flushed, and the palms from which his sweat re-emerged—mine. Finally, my feet began to tremble. I stood, but my legs were wobbling as if there were thunder in the ground.

Kane's aroma, unadulterated by deodorant or aftershave, hovered all about me. I inhaled deeply. Dan Kane smelled like hot buttered toast.

"'Proscribe,'" called a disembodied voice, "'1: to condemn or forbid as harmful or unlawful: prohibit. 2: to publish the name of a person as condemned to death with his property forfeited to the stated.'"

Kane walked back into the kitchen, holding the dictionary. "There you have it, Cham—I mean Franny. The word is 'proscribe.'"

On the wall over Kane's right shoulder hung a portrait of Christ in a plain wooden frame. Those gentle eyes, set off by His long, dark hair, shone with a soft, comforting light.

Over Kane's left shoulder, from a lavish frame adorned with gold rosettes, glowered the jowly face of Archbishop McCoy. No light of any kind emanated from His Excellency.

"Franny?" Kane said tentatively. "Proscribe?"

I remembered what my unfinished business was.

"I'm supposed to ask you who—who your favorite group is," I stammered through a smile as bent as a knot of barbed wire.

"Group?"

"And your favorite color," I added, just before the laughter began.

"Franny—"

My eyes swept left to right over the faces across the room: understanding, confusion, disdain. Proscription. The tremors in the ground resumed and leapt into my body like electricity.

"And... and your middle name—"

As I sank to the floor, laughing hysterically, Dan Kane hesitated. He stared at me in shock for several seconds before he ran forward to help me back up into a chair, enveloping me in his toasty aroma.

"Maybe we've had enough spelling for one day," Kane said.

"Yes, Father."

"It is possible, you know, to be overprepared," he added. "I mean, it can lead to being, well, um . . ."

"Overwrought?" I offered as I stood to leave. He nodded uncertainly.

Father Kane suggested that we skip spelling practice the next day so I could do "whatever boy geniuses do on their days off."

Ha-ha-ha.

Ha-ha-ha. I was fine.

[1994]

BRIDESHEAD REVISITED
Evelyn Waugh

I KNEW SEBASTIAN BY SIGHT LONG BEFORE I MET HIM. THAT WAS unavoidable for, from his first week, he was the most conspicuous man of his year by reason of his beauty, which was arresting, and his eccentricities of behaviour which seemed to know no bounds. My first sight of him was as we passed in the door of Germer's, and, on that occasion, I was struck less by his looks than by the fact that he was carrying a large Teddy-bear.

"That," said the barber, as I took his chair, "was Lord Sebastian Flyte. A *most* amusing young gentleman."

"Apparently," I said coldly.

"The Marquis of Marchmain's second boy. His brother, the Earl of Brideshead, went down last term. Now he was *very* different, a very quiet gentleman, quite like an old man. What do you suppose Lord Sebastian wanted? A hair brush for his Teddy-bear; it had to have very stiff bristles, *not*, Lord Sebastian said, to brush him with, but to threaten him with a spanking when he was sulky. He bought a very nice one with an ivory back and he's having 'Aloysius' engraved on it—that's the bear's name." The man, who, in his time, had had ample chance to tire of undergraduate fantasy, was plainly captivated by him. I, however, remained censorious and subsequent glimpses of Sebastian, driving in a hansom cab and dining at the George in false whiskers, did not soften me, although Collins, who was reading Freud, had a number of technical terms to cover everything.

Nor, when at last we met, were the circumstances propitious. It was shortly before midnight in early March; I had been entertaining the college intellectuals to mulled claret; the fire was roaring, the air of my room heavy with smoke and spice and my mind weary with metaphysics. I threw open my windows and from the quad outside came the not uncommon sounds of bibulous laughter and unsteady steps. A voice said: "Hold up"; another, "Come on"; another, "Plenty of time . . . House . . . till Tom stops ringing"; and another, clearer than the rest, "D'you know I feel most unaccountably unwell. I must leave you a minute," and there appeared at my window the face I knew to be Sebastian's—but not as I had formerly seen it, alive and alight with gaiety; he looked at me for a moment with unseeing eyes and then, leaning forward well into the room, he was sick.

It was not unusual for dinner parties to end that way; there was in fact a recognized tariff on such occasions for the comfort of the scout; we were all learning, by trial and error, to carry our wine. There was also a kind of insane and endearing orderliness about Sebastian's choice, in his extremity, of an open window. But, when all is said, it remained an unpropitious meeting.

[1945]

THE OBJECT OF MY AFFECTION

Stephen McCauley

I WAS TWENTY-FOUR WHEN I MET JOLEY. I'D JUST MOVED TO NEW York to study for a master's in history at Columbia and was living on a loan-padded bank account in a large and filthy apartment in Washington Heights. The first time I saw him across the room at a student-faculty get-together I'm sure I turned away or dropped something; he had exactly the kind of intimidating good looks I found irresistible in my masochistic youth.

I'd like to pretend some powerful intellectual drive propelled me toward graduate school, but the truth is I'd been working for over a year at an inner city day-care center in Boston and was tired of my job and the city, which I'd lived in or around most of my life. I couldn't think of a better way to fund a move than with the assistance of government loans. And New York seemed the likeliest place to go because I was convinced everybody ended up there at some point in life anyway, and I figured I should get it out of the way while I still had the energy.

I went to the Columbia party dressed in a sharkskin suit I'd bought on the street on the Lower East Side, a paisley tie, and a pair of highly polished shoes I'd borrowed from a neighbor. The minute I walked into the plush lounge with its impressive view of Harlem, I realized how off base I was in choosing that outfit, not to mention that course for my life. The room was glutted with a crowd of casually dressed intellectuals devouring each other with condescending smiles. The conversations I overheard in my beeline for the bar revolved around academic journals I'd never read and a cast of celebrity historians the students were apparently on intimate terms with.

When a short, freckled woman standing behind me in the line for the bar asked me what I was studying, I was so intimidated I covered my name tag and quickly told her I wasn't a student. "I'm on the security staff," I said. "I was hired to make sure no one jumps out those windows over there. There's a very high suicide rate in this department."

She pushed her glasses against her freckles and dryly said, "Oh, *really? That's interesting."

"Yes, it's the constant contact with the tragedy of human history— one mistake following the next and no one learning a damned thing from any of it."

"Well, I'll be sure to call you over if I get the urge to jump."

I quickly made my way to a remote corner with two vodka and tonics and tried to look bored or inconspicuous. I'd finished one drink and was chomping on ice cubes when I spotted Joley. He was talking to another teacher, gesticulating dramatically and tossing back his head with humorless laughter. He was just tall enough to stand above most of the people in the room without looking towering and mutant. He had thick silky black hair and a carefully shaggy romantic beard. His best features, however, were his emerald-green eyes which, even across the room, blazed with the kind of fierce intensity I usually associate with the eyes of religious fanatics and mass murderers. He caught me staring at him and stared back in an amused, relaxed way. Here, I thought, was a man who knew how to accept a compliment.

Eventually he made his way to my corner, read my name tag and stuck out his hand.

"George Mullen? How do you do? I'm Robert Joley. I'm your adviser this year. I was hoping I'd see you here. You never know who you'll get a chance to meet at these damned things." He said "damned" the way someone would say "nuisance" to describe a five-million-dollar inheritance.

I mumbled a barely audible hello and started on my second vodka and tonic.

"Actually, George, I just finished reading through your transcript this afternoon. Now let me see if I've got this right—" He put a hand to his forehead with staged precision. "You've recently moved here from Boston. Correct?"

"About a month ago," I said.

"Oh, I do love Boston," he said. "It's so much more civilized than New York. I'd move to Boston in a minute if I had the opportunity."

It was the kind of comment I was always hearing from people who'd sooner have a kidney removed than leave Manhattan. I couldn't tell from Joley's accent if he was a born New Yorker. His voice was curiously flat and toneless, as if he'd had speech lessons or was an anchorman on network news.

"Boston's pretty," I said, "but New York is much more exciting." I'd found nothing exciting in the filth and confusion of those parts of the city I'd been able to afford to visit in the past month. The subway, for example.

"Everything's exciting at a certain age," he said magnanimously.

I was curious to know what age that was but I didn't ask. I tugged at my hideous tie and the sleeves of my suit jacket to try and appear a bit more at ease.

"Now, I don't believe I know specifically what it is you'll be studying, George."

As a matter of fact, neither did I. I was interested in history primarily because I enjoy a good story but I hadn't focused on a particular period or topic. I wasn't, however, about to tell this to my adviser and make a bad impression right off. "Lately," I said, "I've been reading a lot on the unreformed public schools of Victorian England." I'd just read a review of a book on Eton in the Sunday *Times*. "I think I'm becoming obsessed with the subject. It has me enthralled."

"Oh, fantastic, George. I happen to know quite a bit about that. Fascinating." He stepped in closer to me and said, in a low voice, "In *Tom Jones*, Fielding calls the public schools 'the nurseries of all vice and immorality.'"

"I didn't know that," I said. He'd quoted mellifluously, and his breath, which smelled faintly of something antiseptic, washed against my neck, but the quote was from *Joseph Andrews*, not *Tom Jones*. "I'll have to look it up."

"Why bother looking it up? I just told you." He smiled at his generosity and said, "I like your tie."

"I like your beard," I said.

The minute the words were out of my mouth I started praying for an earthquake. One of his colleagues called him off to the other side of the room and I rushed for another pair of drinks. After an hour of solitude, riveted to the floor in my desolate corner, I made a contract with myself: I could leave the party if, and only if, I introduced myself to one person. I'd often made contracts with the kids at the day-care center—they could play at the sink if they stopped beating up on their friends, that kind of thing—and the tactic seemed appropriate in this case.

I picked out a man standing by the window dressed in a Lacoste shirt and cordovan loafers who seemed compatible with my sexual preference if nothing else. I went and stood next to him for a minute or two and then said in a drunken, conspiratorial whisper, "So, do you think we're the only two in the room?"

He turned his face toward me so slowly I thought for a minute he might have a neurobiological disorder. "The only two *what*, may I ask?" he said.

"I'm sorry," I said. "I thought you were Irish. It was just a guess, a hunch, if you know what I mean. Great to meet you."

My peers were leaving in small chatty groups, most accompanied by a doddering teacher holding court. I walked out of the lounge thinking I had no choice but to admit defeat and quit school immediately, before the first day began.

[1987]

LIFE STORY

Tennessee Williams

After you've been to bed together for the first time,
without the advantage or disadvantage of any prior acquaintance,
the other party very often says to you,
Tell me about yourself, I want to know all about you,
what's your story? And you think maybe they really and truly do

sincerely want to know your life story, and so you light up
a cigarette and begin to tell it to them, the two of you
lying together in completely relaxed positions
like a pair of rag dolls a bored child dropped on a bed.

You tell them your story, or as much of your story
as time or a fair degree of prudence allows, and they say,
    Oh, oh, oh, oh, oh,
each time a little more faintly, until the oh
is just an audible breath, and then of course

there's some interruption. Slow room service comes up
with a bowl of melting ice cubes, or one of you rises to pee
and gaze at himself with mild astonishment in the bathroom mirror.
And then, the first thing you know, before you've had time
to pick up where you left off with your enthralling life story,
they're telling you *their* life story, exactly as they'd intended
    to all along,

and you're saying, Oh, oh, oh, oh, oh,
each time a little more faintly, the vowel at last becoming
no more than an audible sigh,
as the elevator, halfway down the corridor and a turn to the left,
draws one last, long, deep breath of exhaustion
and stops breathing forever. Then?

Well, one of you falls asleep
and the other one does likewise with a lighted cigarette in his mouth,
and that's how people burn to death in hotel rooms.

[1956]

THE FOLDING STAR

Alan Hollinghurst

IT WAS CLEAR ON THE STREETS, TOO, AS I WALKED OVER TO THE Altidores', that things had changed: a flat-footed straggler with his shirt-tails hanging out came panting past me and stopped, wincing with the stitch; two truants tugged off their ties before slipping into a video shop; in a sudden sally from a side-street a games-kitted crocodile lurched at a run into my path, headed by a manic bald master. It was the first day and there were the children caught up already in the severe rhythms of school, and looking back, like conscripts on a ship, to the lazy shore of home. For a moment I shared the truants' defiance and guilt and my heart raced with a long-forgotten panicky anticipation: I had to assert myself against the obscure medicinal hollowness of school. And of course my first assignation with Luc loomed and made me feel half master and half victim.

His mother got hold of me first, and took me into the dining room. She hoped I didn't mind coming to the house, it seemed better discipline than sending Luc across town to me—and then she knew where he was. I was already imagining the squeaking board that gave away her presence at the door. She went on with a number of blunt and incoherent instructions, which I barely took in—I was pretending I hadn't seen him, just at the moment I entered the hall, behind his mother's back, skidding through the kitchen, a towel round his neck, a glimpse of his bare heels, a vision of his undomestic size and energy.

She left me in the darkly panelled room, among the family portraits. I waited a minute under their humourless gaze, one above the other, prudent, black-bosomed, as if they had all been painted in widowhood. Feeling faintly culpable and unfit for responsibility, I went to the long window and looked out on the garden, a high-walled strip that ended in a canal with swans idling past and a little angular gazebo above the water, where I pictured Luc smoking or waiting for a tryst. Mrs. Altidore's work was less evident in this room, just a kind of tasselled runner on the sideboard. Then I pulled out a chair and discovered the terrible industry of the seat.

There were footsteps, no voices, crossing the hall, and their brief hanging back to let the other enter first showed me they were both nervous too. Mother and son, side by side: I sensed the treaty between them and the unresolved cross-purpose.

"This is Luc," she said. "Mr. Manners."

He was pushing back his hair and his hand was damp when he shook mine.

"Hello."

"Hello!" How old-fashionedly keen I was.

And he nodded, so that his hair fell forward again. Through the coming hour I would see that tumbling forelock dry from bronze to gold, and get to know the different ways he mastered it, the indolent sweep, the brainstorming grapple, the barely effectual toss, and how long the intervals were of forward slither and lustrous collapse. But for the moment, when we were left alone, I didn't altogether look at him; my eyes fixed uncomprehendingly on the sideboard, a hideous epergne, a sugar dredger, a tantalus of brandy.

He said, "My mother's going to bring some coffee," the voice light and mildly interrogative, the accent educated. Then I looked. He was lean and broad-shouldered in an old blue shirt; and I liked his big flattish backside as he walked past me, though his loose cotton trousers gave nothing else away. He was as tall as me (I could imagine him saying he was taller, and a laughing challenge, back to back). Did he understand that I was weighing and measuring him like this, or possibly envisage the tingle of desire that ran up my back when I saw his brown bare insteps between turn-up and low-cut moccasin? It was hard to know if something vain and mistrustful in his look was more than the ordinary wariness of a boy with his teacher, or of people starting cold at knowing each other.

To me of course he wasn't quite new, though when he took his place on the far side of the table and waited for me to begin I could hardly keep from telling him how different he was from his picture, how much odder and better. In his father's generation his features might have been thought ugly or exaggerated, though now they had come into fashion and could be admitted as wonderful in their own way; he must have taken from his father the long nose and high cheekbones which gave him the air of a blond Aztec. His eyes were narrow and colourless—his mother's lost look given a new caution and sharpness; while his long mouth seemed burdened with involuntary expressiveness, the thick lips opening, when later I twisted a smile out of him, to show strong sexy canines and high gums. His upper lip was almost too heavy, a puckering outward curl, with no downward dimple in the fingermark beneath the nose, where it had a straight edge, as if finished off impatiently with a palette-knife. There was something engrossing, even slightly repellent, about the whole feature.

His mother knocked and brought two coffees in with a self-denying expression, as if to say that this would be her last intrusion on the serious work we had to do. Then the conversation made its faltering beginnings, and ran on for minute after minute, with topics artificially encouraged gaining a brief involuntary momentum before dying like an old engine in which too much confidence had been placed. We spoke about the geography of Belgium, the relative merits of the western plain and the south-easterly heights, and discussed the Flemish/Walloons question without reaching any very deep or new conclusions. It was a puzzling experience—I was fascinated by him, yet carrying on as though I'd been trapped with a bore at a cocktail party. Perhaps he really was a bore; there was no reason he shouldn't be, whatever his fretful mother had said. Or was I expecting too much too soon, and ignoring his steady merits, the schoolboy's vacant valuing of knowledge for its own sake? I felt I needed to find out about him, or like some subtle interrogator to beguile him into unnoticed indiscretions; I was slightly miffed when he started to give things away without much bother or self-importance.

He was looking sunned and well, so I asked him about his recent spell out at the seaside. He had been to the villa of a former schoolfriend, just over the French border, right on the beach at a village called St Ernest-aux-Sablonnières, to which, he told me confidently, the saint's body had been brought after his fatal crusade. Patrick something was his great friend there, another rich kid I guessed, and they had often been together to this beach-house in the long holidays when the something family went out there. This time the fine weather on the very brink of the new term had tempted the boys to go there for a few days alone; or so I thought, and jealously hoped, until it emerged that there had also been a girl with them.

I fell into a rhythm of apparently pointless questions, so as to stretch his vocabulary; and under cover of these I went stalking through that seaside idyll that there had never been the remotest question of my sharing. First, how had they got there? In his friend Patrick's car. Ah, and what was that? A Mini! Oh; and what was the house like? It was white, it had only one floor, and its roof was flat. A verandah with white pillars ran all along the front. To my surprise he called it a stoa. Below the house there was a garden with trees that leant over and a gate with two or three steps going down on to the dunes. The nearest house was a hundred metres off. And what of the inside? There were at least four bedrooms (so perfect chastity could conceivably have been preserved). We itemised the linen, the duvet-covers in red and green, the sheets made from an uncertain fabric. The furniture there was built out of pine and oak; there were many books on wildlife and ornithology. The theme of birds was continued on the cups and plates, and on various other items in the kitchen, which he considered a delightful room. I wanted to get back to the night hours, and ask him what he dreamed about when the noise of the waves had lulled him to sleep; but something held me back. I felt I could pry no further just now, though he rose to all these challenges with only brief hesitations and a certain chilly pride. What had they done? They had walked, read, studied indeed, discussed various matters. Such as? Such as . . . pollution, radio drama, the effect of wage agreements. They sounded like the dreariest people on earth. (They sounded like us.) Had they gone in the sea? Yes, although the water was quite cold. Then what had he worn to do so? A slip. Swimming-trunks, did he mean, or shorts? Trunks. And what colour were they? They were black. As it happened, he'd forgotten his own and had to borrow Patrick's, and they were too large. So he couldn't keep them on? Oh he could, but it wasn't easy...What, um, what had he *read*? He had read *Great Expectations* and something by Gramsci! (He seemed full of ideas on the latter but I kept bringing him firmly to Pip, Magwitch and Herbert Pocket.)

When a little over an hour had elapsed there was another quick knock and Mrs. Altidore stepped in and looked from one to the other of us, as if expecting a decision. There was a moment's silence. Then she asked Luc how it had gone, and he nodded and shrugged, accustomed to evading her fuss. I told her that he had very good English and she said, "I know." She then had Luc show me out, which he did with a telling mixture of reluctance and formality. I shook his big strong hand and he nodded his forelock forward and curtly said goodbye.

Out in the street I felt almost nothing. I didn't like to inspect my motives—I walked on quite briskly, looking about appreciatively, like someone at ease with himself and not denying a disappointment. Though the question that insisted on forming, whether I had really come all this way for *that*.

[1994]

LOVE! VALOUR! COMPASSION!

Terrence McNally

(*They are both looking out across the lake to Ramon.*)

JAMES: My brother has always had a good-looking man in his life.

BUZZ: Thank you.

JAMES: I beg your pardon?

BUZZ: He didn't tell you? It was when he first came to this country. Short and sweet. Six months, tops.

JAMES: I'm sorry. What happened?

BUZZ: We were both very young. I was too needy. He wasn't needy enough.

JAMES: I don't think John can love anyone.

BUZZ: Now you tell me!

JAMES: Perhaps one of us had better go out there and tell Ramon.

BUZZ: I'll let you break it to him. I don't think I'm his type.

JAMES: I don't think either of us is.
(*They are both still staring out across the lake to Ramon on the raft.*)
I enjoy looking, though.
(*Buzz and James sigh.*)

BUZZ: Is there a British equivalent for "machismo"?

JAMES: No. None at all. Maybe Glenda Jackson.

BUZZ: Do you have a boyfriend over there?

JAMES: Not anymore. What about you?

BUZZ (*shaking his head*): When the going gets tough, weak boyfriends get going. Or something like that.

JAMES: I can't honestly say I'm minding. Last acts are depressing and generally one long solo.

BUZZ: They don't have to be.
(*Buzz finally looks at James.*)
How sick are you?

JAMES: I think I'm in pretty good nick, but my reports read like something out of Nostradamus.
(*He looks at Buzz.*)
I should have died six months ago.

BUZZ: Try eighteen. Do you have any lesions?

JAMES: Only one, and I've had it for nearly a year.

BUZZ: Where is it?

JAMES: In a very inconvenient spot.

BUZZ: They're all inconvenient. May I see it?

JAMES: It's—All right.
(*He pulls up his shirt and lets Buzz see the lesion.*)
I have a lesbian friend in London who's the only other person who's ever asked to see it. I was quite astonished when she did. Touched, actually. Mortified, too, of course. But mainly touched. Somebody loves me, even if it's not the someone I've dreamed of. A little love from a woman who works in the box office at the Lyric Hammersmith is better than none. Are you through?
(*Buzz kisses the lesion.*)

JAMES: Gwyneth didn't go that far. It doesn't disgust you?

BUZZ: It's going to be me.

JAMES: You don't know that.

BUZZ: Yes I do.

JAMES: You learn to make friends with them. Hello, little lesion. Not people you like especially, but people you've made your peace with.

BUZZ: You're very nice, you know.

JAMES: Frankly, I don't see how I can afford not to be.

BUZZ: No, I mean it.

JAMES: So are you.

BUZZ: I didn't mean to interrupt your reading.

JAMES: It was getting too intense. They just outed George and Ira Gershwin.

BUZZ: Wait till they get to Comden and Green. Would you like me to bring you a real drink down? I know where they hide the good liquor.

JAMES: An ice-cold martini. Very dry. With a twist.

BUZZ: Is that going to be good for you?

JAMES: Of course not.

BUZZ: Does this make me an enabler?

JAMES: No, but it makes me your slave for life. I'll snitch a frock out of the National Theatre storage for you. Something of Dame Edith Evans'.

BUZZ: What's the matter?

JAMES: I'm waiting for you to tell me she was gay.

BUZZ: She wasn't, actually. One of the two British actresses who isn't. I think Deborah Kerr is the other one. But all the rest— galloping lezzies!
(*He goes. James looks after him and does not resume reading for quite some time.*)

[1995]

41

THE FIRST KISS

Robert Peters

at first
a feeling like
silk, then
a slight motion
of lip on lip
and breathing.
I take your
lower lip
into my mouth,
delight
in its blood-round
softness, re-
lease it. we kiss.
your tongue
explores; for
the first time
it touches mine:
tip and surface,
root and vein
our eyes open.

[1973]

REPRISE *Edmund White*

JIM GRADY CALLED MY MOTHER AND INVITED HIMSELF OVER ON Saturday evening to watch *The Perry Como Show* on television. He informed her he was an absolute fanatic about Como, that he considered Como's least glance or tremolo incomparably cool, and that he especially admired his long-sleeved golfer's sweaters with the low-slung yoke necks, three buttons at the waist, coarse spongy weave and bright colors. My mother told me about these odd enthusiasms; she was puzzled by them because she thought that fashion concerned women alone and that even over women its tyranny extended only to clothes, certainly not to ways of moving, smiling or singing. "I wouldn't want to imitate anyone else," she said with her little mirthless laugh of self-congratulation and disbelieving shake of her head. "I like being me just fine, thank you very much."

"He's not the first young person to swoon over a pop star," I informed her out of my infinite world-weariness.

"Men don't swoon over men, dear," Mother reminded me, peering at me over the tops of her glasses. Now that I unscrambled the signals she was emitting, I see how contradictory they were. She said she admired the sensitivity of a great dancer such as Nijinsky, and she'd even given me his biography to make sure I knew the exact perverse composition of that sensitivity: "What a tragic life. Of course he ended up psychotic with paranoid delusions, martyr complex and degenerative ataxia." She'd assure me, with snapping eyes and carnivorous smile, that she liked men to be men and a boy to be all boy (as who does not), although the hearty heartlessness of making such a declaration to her willowy, cake-baking, harp-playing son thoroughly eluded her. Nor would she have tolerated a real boy's beer brawls, bloody noses or stormy fugues. She wanted an obedient little gentleman who would sit placidly in a dark suit when he wasn't helping his mother until, at the appropriate moment and with no advance fuss, he would marry a plain Christian girl whose unique vocation would be the perpetual adoration of her mother-in-law.

At last, after our dispirited Saturday night supper, Jim Grady arrived, just in time for a slice of my devil's food cake and *The Perry Como Show*. What a coincidence that I'd chosen the Como show at random but that Como really was Jim's hero! My sister skulked off to her room to polish her hockey stick and read through fan-magazine articles on Mercedes McCambridge and Barbara Stanwyck. Jim belted back the six-pack he'd brought along and drew our attention with repulsive connoisseurship to every cool Como mannerism. I now realize that maybe Como was the first singer who'd figured out that the TV lens represented twenty million horny women dateless on Saturday night; he looked searchingly into its glass eye and warbled with the calm certainty of his seductive charm.

As a homosexual, I understood the desire to possess an admired man, but I was almost disgusted by Jim's ambition to imitate him. My mother saw men as nearly faceless extras who surrounded the diva, a woman; I regarded men as the stars; but both she and I were opposed to all forms of masculine self-fabrication, she because she considered it unbecomingly narcissistic, I because it seemed a sacrilegious parody of the innate superiority of a few godlike men. Perhaps I was just jealous that Jim was paying more attention to Como than to me.

Emboldened by beer, Jim called my mother by her first name, which I'm sure she found flattering, since it suggested he saw her as a woman rather than as a parent. She drank one of her many highballs with him, sitting beside him on the couch, and for an instant I coldly appraised my own mother as a potential rival, but she lost interest in him when he dared to shush her during a bit of the singer's studied patter. In those days before the veneration of pop culture, unimaginative highbrows such as my mother and I swooned over opera, foreign films of any sort and "problem plays" such as *The Immoralist* and *Tea and Sympathy*, but in spite of ourselves we were guiltily drawn to television with a mindless, vegetable-like tropism best named by the vogue word of the period, "apathy." And yet we certainly thought it beneath us to *study* mere entertainment.

Jim was so masculine in the way he held a Lucky cupped between his thumb and middle finger and kept another unlit behind his ear, he was so inexpressive, so devoid of all gesture, that when he stood up to go, shook his head like a wet dog and said, "Damn! I've had one too many for the road," he was utterly convincing. My mother said, "Do you want me to drive you home?" Jim laughed insultingly and said, "I think you're feeling no pain yourself. I'd better stay over, Delilah, if you have an extra bed."

My mother was much more reluctant to put Jim up than I'd anticipated. "I don't know, I could put my girdle back on . . ." Had she picked up the faint sex signal winking back and forth between Jim and her son? Perhaps she worried how it might look to Mr. Grady: drunk son spends night at Delilah's apartment—and such a son, the human species at its peak of physical fitness, mouth open, eyes shifting, Adam's apple working.

At last we were alone, and operatically I shed my clothes in a puddle at my feet, but Jim, undressing methodically, whispered, "You should hang your clothes up or your mother might think we were up to some sort of monkey business." Hot tears sprang to my eyes, but they dried as I looked at the long torso being revealed, with its small, turned waist and the wispy hairs around the tiny brown nipples. His legs were pale because he'd worn jeans on the construction site, but he must have worn them low. For an instant he sat down to pull off his heavy white socks, and his shoulder muscles played under the overhead light with all the demonic action of a Swiss music box, the big kind with its works under glass.

He lay back with a heavy-lidded, cool expression I suspected was patterned on Como's, but I didn't care, I was even pleased he wanted to impress me as I scaled his body, felt his great warm arms around me, tasted the Luckies and Bud on his lips, saw the sharp focus in his eyes fade into a blur. "Hey," he whispered, and he smiled at me as his hands cupped my twenty-six-inch waist and my hot penis planted its flag on the stony land of his perfect body. "Hey," he said, hitching me higher and deeper into his presence.

Soon after that I came down with mononucleosis, the much-discussed "kissing disease" of our time, although I'd kissed almost no one but Jim. I was tired and depressed. I dragged myself with difficulty from couch to bed, but at the same time I was so lonely and frustrated that I looked down from the window at every man or boy walking past and willed him to look up, see me, join me, but the will was weak.

Jim called one afternoon and we figured out he could come by the next evening when my mother was going somewhere with my sister. I warned him he could catch mono if he kissed me, but I was proud after all he did kiss me long and deep. Until now the people I'd had sex with were boys at camp who pretended to hypnotize each other or married men who cruised the Howard Street Elevator toilets and drove me down to the beach in station wagons filled with their children's toys. Jim was the first man who took off his clothes, held me in his arms, looked me in the eye and said, "Hey."

I was bursting with my secret, all the more so because mononucleosis had reduced my world to the size of our apartment and the books I was almost too weak to hold (that afternoon it had been Oscar Wilde's *Lady Windermere's Fan*). In the evening my mother was washing dishes and I was drying, but I kept sitting down to rest. She said, "Mr. Grady and I are thinking about getting married." The words just popped out of my mouth: "Then it will have to be a double wedding." My brilliant repartee provoked not a laugh but an inquisition, which had many consequences for me over the years, both good and bad. The whole story of my homosexual adventures came out, my father was alerted, I was sent off to boarding school and a psychiatrist—my entire life changed.

My mother called up Jim Grady and boozily denounced him as a pervert and a child molester, although I'd assured her I'd been the one to seduce him. I did not see him again until almost forty years later in Paris. My mother, who'd become tiny, wise and sober with age, had had several decades to get used to the idea of my homosexuality (and my sister's as it turned out). She had run into Jim Grady twice in the last three years and warned me he'd become maniacally stingy, so much so he'd wriggle out of a drinks date if he thought he'd have to pay.

[1995]

SPONTANEOUS COMBUSTION

David B. Feinberg

I HATED ALL OF HIS FRIENDS, AND HE COULDN'T STAND ANY OF MINE; every chance meeting was fraught with peril. It was safest when we stuck to our apartments and ordered out Chinese, rented old horror flicks, and had copious amounts of sexual intercourse.

The snideness of his friends' responses was unparalleled in the history of queendom. Roger's friends discussed accessories constantly, along with fashion utensils, sexual appliances, household demographics, makeup secrets, interior deconstructionism, and skin-care secrets. They all worked in the madcap world of design: remixing music videos, deranging window displays, bending hair, slinging hash, filing teeth, and so on.

My friend Cameron didn't fare any better with Roger. The three of us met in a Mexican restaurant. Cameron chose that moment to inform Roger that Madonna's latest blasphemous video had changed his life. Cameron then made us move to another table because the lighting was rather unflattering. For some reason that escapes me, Cameron grated on Roger's nerves, although Roger was kind enough not to bring it to my immediate attention.

[1991]

THE WEEKEND

Peter Cameron

LYLE WOKE UP WITH A BLACK EYE. HE HAD NEVER HAD A BLACK EYE before. He stood for a while, looking at it in the bathroom mirror. It was such an ugly thing: the purple and yellow stain of it on his face. He wanted to stay away from everyone until it disappeared, but he knew that was impossible, so he went down to breakfast.

Roland was ensconced in his high chair at the table. Marian was sitting next to him, feeding him some yogurt. "Oh, my God," she said, as Lyle entered the room. "Your eye!"

"Yes," said Lyle. He sat down.

"Does it hurt?" asked Marian.

"No," said Lyle. "I'd rather not talk about it."

"Of course," said Marian. "Here, let me get you some coffee."

"I'll get it," said Lyle. He stood up and poured himself a cup of coffee. "Where's John?" he asked.

"Where do you think?" said Marion. She nodded toward the garden.

Lyle sat at the table for a moment, drinking his coffee, watching Marian feed Roland. "Could I do that?" he asked. "Could I feed him?"

"Of course," said Marian. "Do you want Uncle Lyle to feed you?" she asked Roland.

Roland seemed not to care.

"Here," Marian said, handing the spoon to Lyle. "He's hungry. Just give him little spoonfuls till he won't take anymore. He'll turn his head away when he's had enough."

Lyle held the first spoonful out to Roland, who eyed it, and Lyle, for a moment, and then somewhat reluctantly opened his mouth. Lyle gently inserted the spoon. "Good boy," he said.

Marian watched them and said, "It's a lovely day. A little cooler than yesterday."

"Good," said Lyle.

"We have nothing planned. Just a lazy day."

"Good," said Lyle.

They sat in silence, intent on the feeding of Roland. Finally he turned his head away. "Finished?" asked Lyle. "No more?"

"You did very well," said Marian. "Let me wipe his face off." She got up and dampened a cloth.

"Let me," said Lyle. He wiped the yogurt from around Roland's small mouth. Then he picked him up, out of the high chair, and held him against his chest. "Can I ask you a question?" he said to Marian.

"Of course you may," said Marian.

"Did you like Robert?"

Marian thought for a moment. "No," she said. "I don't think I did. But it's hard to know, because, well, I didn't really get to know him, did I? It was all so strained yesterday, and then with his running off like that. Why do you ask? Lyle, tell me. What happened last night?"

"Robert had the feeling you didn't like him," said Lyle.

"Did he? That's a shame."

"Actually, he said he overheard you telling John you didn't like him."

Marian didn't say anything for a moment, and then she said, "Why did you do that?"

"What?" asked Lyle.

"Ask me the question, when you knew the answer. Why did you try to trap me like that?"

"I didn't mean to trap you," said Lyle.

"You didn't?" asked Marian. "Then what did you mean?"

"I don't know," said Lyle. "I wanted to know what you'd tell me. What you'd say to me."

"You didn't think I'd tell you the truth?" asked Marian.

"I didn't know," said Lyle. "I'm confused. Yesterday you told me you liked him."

"Well, I did, yesterday. At least I was trying hard to. And I still would be, today, if he were here. Besides, I don't make decisions about whether I like people or not on the basis of a few hours in their company."

"I think Robert thought you had."

"I'm sorry he thought that. Is that why he left? Because he thought I didn't like him?"

"He didn't think it. He knew it. Or thought he knew it. He heard you say it."

"Well, I'm sorry," said Marian. "I was trying to be nice to him. I was trying to like him. I'm sorry if he overheard me say something that hurt him."

"You don't have to be sorry," said Lyle.

"Oh?" said Marian. "Don't I? Isn't that what you're saying? That this is all my fault?"

"No," said Lyle. "Not at all. It's my fault, if anyone's. He didn't leave because you didn't like him. He left because he thought *I* didn't like him. Or love him. He wanted me to tell him I loved him, and I wouldn't. So he panicked, and ran away."

"He sounds like a spoiled baby," said Marian.

"He is," said Lyle. "We all are, deep down. Some of us are just better at hiding it than others."

"I disagree," said Marian. "I don't think it's a matter of hiding anything. I think it's a matter of learning how to behave responsibly and respectfully. Learning how to consider other people. You don't run off into the night just because someone won't tell you that they love you. That's hardly the behavior of a rational adult."

"Yes," said Lyle. "I know it isn't."

"You need to find someone, Lyle—in time, at the right time—some adult, somebody who understands who you are. Robert may have been very sweet, but I don't think he was that person. Do you?"

"No," said Lyle. "But—"

"But what?"

"I liked him. Nevertheless, I liked him very much."

"Well, of course you liked him. I understand that: He wasn't stupid, was he, and he was good-looking, and he adored you. It's no wonder you liked him. But that doesn't mean he was right for you, does it?"

"No," said Lyle. "In fact, that's what I told him, last night."

"You told him that?"

"Yes. He asked me."

"Well, I suppose he deserved it then, if he asked you. In that case, I think you should just forget about him and have a pleasant day. The weekend's only half over, you know. You're not leaving until this evening, are you?"

"Yes," said Lyle. "Or late this afternoon."

"Good," said Marian. "I thought maybe we could take a picnic lunch up the river in the punt. How does that sound?"

"That sounds fine," said Lyle. There was a pause, and then Lyle said, "What punt?"

"I meant the rowboat," said Marian.

"Then why did you call it a punt?"

"I don't know," said Marian. "I suppose because I like the idea of a punt. I like to think of it as a punt. Is that a crime?"

"No," said Lyle. "Of course not."

"Then why did you correct me? Do you think I romanticize everything?"

"A little," said Lyle. "Sometimes."

"Oh," said Marian. "Well, I suppose you're right. But I don't see the harm in it. Really, I don't. It doesn't hurt anyone, does it? To call a rowboat a punt?"

"No," said Lyle, "of course it doesn't. It's just that between us, between you and me, I . . . I see no need. I want things to be honest between us, and clear."

"I thought they were," said Marian. "Have I been deluding myself about that as well?"

They were silent a moment. "Is he sleeping?" Marian asked. She meant Roland.

"No," said Lyle. He looked down at Roland. "He's wide awake. Alert as can be. He seems very alert for his age."

"Does he?" said Marian. "Do you really think so?"

"Well, as far as I can tell. I don't know many babies. But look at him watching me. He's definitely thinking something."

"I think it's your eye," said Marian. "It's quite colorful. Does it hurt?"

"No," said Lyle. "A little. Yes."

"Aren't you supposed to put steak on it? I think I've got some I could defrost."

"Don't bother," said Lyle. "It's fine."

Marian reached out her arms. Lyle handed the baby to her. She held him and looked down at him. "Sometimes I'm scared," she said.

"Of what?"

"Of Roland. Of how much I love him. He keeps me sane, and alive. And I think he shouldn't. That it's not right. That it's I who should do that for him."

"Well, can't it work both ways?" asked Lyle.

Marian didn't answer. She was crying. Lyle watched her. He did not know what to say.

[1994]

MARTIN AND JOHN

Dale Peck

LATER, MONTHS LATER, HE AND MY MOTHER WERE MARRIED, AND she had me put away my father's condoling picture forever. Martin and I never had sex again; and once, after tousling my hair, he sat up quickly and said he couldn't do that any longer either, and he left my bedroom. Still wanting him, I would look at him for long periods of time, staring at him through his newspaper until he would drop it tensely and look back at me, softly, sharply, fearfully, always with love and sadness, and once or twice with lust also, but each time he only shrugged it, all of it, away.

The marriage didn't last because my mother only loved him for helping her to overcome drinking and my father's specter. I never saw her fight with him; she only drifted further and further away, and grew more silent until one day all she could say was "I'm sorry—" and he moved out without protest. Later I learned that they'd said things when I wasn't there, had fought and made up, fucked, talked about me, done the dishes and things like that, lived a separate life while I was out; but then I only hated my mother for sending Martin away even though I loved him more than she. I yelled at her that I would never forgive her if she didn't bring him back, nor would I accept anyone else, for that is what I believed she'd do: go find someone else. With the cruelty of adolescence I screamed, "You're just a slut!" For a moment I stared at the air, as if I could see the word I'd just hurled at my mother. Then she slapped me hard, twice, and said, "Only when I'm dead and gone can you say things like that about me. But while I'm alive you make damn good and sure you mind your place!" On her final words, her voice rose to a scream. I jumped up and down, my arms flying out and hitting the walls so hard that a picture frame filled with family shots fell to the floor—my father, my mother, me; and, still tucked in the frame in front of the glass, new configurations featuring Martin and the two of us. "I loved him!" I yelled, pointing at the broken glass and scattered pictures. "I loved him! And he loved me!" "Shut up!" my mother shrieked. She grabbed me by the hair and threw me down. I lay there and looked up at her. Her face was twisted with rage and disgust. "Don't you ever say that again." I stared at her, my mouth open, tasting blood though I wasn't bleeding. "Get away from me, you foul boy," she said, and turned away. If sleeping with Martin had taught me anything, it had taught me about desire, and I yelled at her retreating form, "You're just pissed because he got what you wanted." She turned, and I saw the shocked expression on her face, and then, before she could hit me again, I ran away.

I was too angry to admit my grief or guilt, and choked on the apology I knew she deserved. Weeks went by and we didn't speak, and I heard it through a friend that Martin had moved from town. Only when my mother dragged out my father's picture did I realize how deeply I'd cut. But the alcohol was gone and the only addiction was to a dead man's memory, and I no more had the cure to that than she could stifle my own sobs for Martin, so I used my pillow to do it to save her any more pain; she clinging to her picture, I to my pillow, we both searched for the essences of men long gone.

[1993]

THE MUTE BOY
Ethan Mordden

HE WAS NOT DEAF, ONLY MUTE, APPARENTLY THE REVERSE OF THE usual condition; even a fluke, for all I could guess, for I never asked. He was proud of his ability to cope with his impairment but, if not ashamed of it, reticent about it. His many friends protected him—crowded him in theatres, blocked and ran passes for him in bars, sat in on his dinners with new friends, sounded for him in banks and restaurants. His family constantly found reasons to come east and check up on him, bring him things, kiss him. I, who was to turn thirty before I dared embrace my father and have never done more than shake hands with my brothers, was dazzled. Still, I wondered how much protection one needs. Mac's friends insistently set him up with Good Husband Material; their dinner parties looked like the waiting room at Yenta the Matchmaker's. And Mac's family had their version, prodding him to Come Home and Settle Down— meaning, translated from the straight, "Give up the rebellious gay phase and do what is done."

But Mac loved the city. He loved crowds and dinners and doing eight things every evening. "Do you realize?" he had written in one of his earliest letters, "that there are probably a million gays in New York? Allowing for variables of looks, spirit, vocation, and bad habits, each of us may have a thousand ideal mates within immediate geography. We need but look."

What can you project without a voice in this town of the insinuating opener and whipcrack reply? You might show optimism, hesitation, disappointment, pain—and all too clearly. Speakers grow up learning to develop or hide their emotions; Mac had learned only to display his. Thus did he speak, as he claimed. Better, he charmed. And I mean strangers. Belligerent strangers. Even belligerent, tough strangers on a mean bad day.

I went walking with him one afternoon when he had just received news about an aunt who had cancer; like a puppy, Mac perked up when you walked him. I'm a champion at distracting wounded comrades— when all else fails, I start a fight—but Mac was half in a daze, and blundered into fresh-laid concrete on Forty-ninth Street, east of Park. One of the masons, foully irate, came over to berate him. Before I could intervene with my usual exacerbating ruckus, Mac stopped me, indicating the laborer with the philosopher's upheld index finger and himself with a down-turned thumb.

"He's right and I'm wrong," I sounded, dubiously, for Mac. He showed us the sidewalk, ran a hand over his eyes, and chided the hand with a look. "I should have been watching where I was going."

As the laborer blankly surveyed this latest charade of the Manhattan streets, Mac tore off a message for him.

"'I have had bad news,'" the man read out. "'I'm sorry.'" He looked at Mac. "Family news, huh?"

Mac nodded.

"Yeah, well . . . yeah, sure." He shifted his stance and patted Mac's shoulder. "It'll be all right. I'm sorry, too. For yelling."

Mac hit his chest with a fist and shook his head. "No," I sounded. "It was my fault."

"No—"

Mac hit himself again.

"*No.*" The man grabbed Mac by the shoulders. "No, you . . . look . . . I gotta get back to work." He touched Mac's nose and gave him a quarter. "Be a good boy, now."

Mac smiled and nodded.

"Right," I said, after we had walked a bit. "I've been in New York for seven years and I've seen, I think, everything. But did that really happen?"

Mac shrugged benignly.

"*He gave you a quarter!*"

"People like me," Mac wrote. "I'm nice."

"What's the secret of nice?" I wondered aloud.

"Forgiving," he wrote.

He could have used somewhat more in height and weight, no doubt; it doesn't do to be quite so boyish after twenty-six. Yet he made it work, for his short and thin suited the grin and the nod. He was the kind of man who could grow a moustache and no one would notice—would see it, even. He was the eternal kid, tirelessly seeking his mate. Fastidious, he wanted true love or nothing. But love is scarce even when forgiveness makes you nice, and I wondered what Mac did to fill in meanwhile, till one afternoon when Dennis Savage and I were hacking around in Mac's apartment and Mac pulled out the world's largest collection of porn magazines.

He did it, typically, to stop a war. Dennis Savage was cranky (as usual) and began to growl at me about something or other. Who knows, now, what? My taste in men? My dislike of travel? The Charge of the Light Brigade? Anyway:

"I'm going to get a huge dog," says Dennis Savage. "And you know what I'll train him to do?"

Mac touched us urgently, him then me. "Please don't fight," I sounded; adding, for myself, "Okay."

"Bite up your ass," Dennis Savage concluded.

"You don't need a dog for that, from what I hear."

He rose, fuming like Hardy when Laurel puts a fish in his pants, and Mac got between us, scribbling a cease-fire: "Sit down to play Fantasy." Bemused, we held our peace as he hauled stacks of magazines out of a closet. "I usually play by myself," he mimed to my sound, "but it works in groups, too." He handed us each a number, prime porn. "Browse and choose," he wrote. "Each gets anyone he wants for one night."

"Get him," said Dennis Savage.

"Mac wrote a note just for him: "Pretend!"

"Where did all this porn come from?" I asked. "It's like the Decadent Studies Room at the Library of Congress."

Mac went through an elaborate mime. "I threw up on the bureau of my aunt?" suggested Dennis Savage.

Mac made a wry face as he picked up the pad. "It keeps me off the streets," he wrote.

"Strange men give him quarters," I added. "They touch his nose."

"He forgives," Dennis Savage noted, "and his kisses are as sweet as the bottom inch of a Dannon cup." Innocence is Dennis Savage's party.

Mac reverently showed us a spread entitled "The Boys of Soho." Writing "This one's my fave," he pointed out a dark-haired chap of about twenty-five, standing nude, arms folded across his stomach. There was nothing splendid about his looks or proportions, but something arresting somewhere; his face, you thought; you searched it, found nothing, but kept looking. Amid a load of musclemen, hung boys, and surly toughs, here was a man of no special detail but an attitude of sleaze too personable to ignore. I imagine evil looks like this.

"'Nick,'" I read out. "'A typical Soho boy with an air of fun and a taste for the finer things.' What does that mean, I wonder?"

"Hepatitis B on the first date," Dennis Savage answered.

Mac mimed, and I sounded: "Do you think he would respond to a letter?"

"Mac, you wouldn't fall in love like that! What would your family say?"

"Just for a night," Mac mimed, then, by pad: "How would you contact such a person?"

"We wouldn't know," said Dennis Savage, "so forget it."

"You could write him a letter in care of the photographer," I put in. "Or even call the photographer and ask—"

"You bonehead!" Dennis Savage pointed out.

"Let the kid have some fun. Why should he go through life only imagining where every path leads? Everyone alive who isn't a coward or a creep deserves one glorious night."

"Which are you? Coward or creep?"

"Glorious."

He waved this nonsense away and concentrated on Mac. "I'm going to set you up with some very excellent Italian accountants in the West Seventies. They make the best husbands, believe me. Always remember The Three Advantages of the Italian beau: hairy chest, volcanic thighs, and the commitment of a Pope."

"*Volcanic thighs?*" I howled. "And dare I ask where the lava comes out?"

Slowly he turned. He regarded me. He was stern. "You know, you should take care where you go. Fag-bashing incidents have been reported in this area."

"Such as where?"

"Such as in this apartment in about three seconds."

"I dream of Nick," Mac had written, and now showed us his little pad. "I think it's always Nick."

"Another good boy goes wrong," said Dennis Savage. "Is that why you left Racine? To meet Nicks?"

Mac gazed at the photograph. "He's such a beautiful dude," I sounded, watching Mac's face.

"Will you shut up?" Dennis Savage roared.

"It wasn't me."

Porn models are surprisingly easy to meet—as if their photos were meant as credentials for work. Despite Dennis Savage's reservations, I helped Mac make contact with Nick. This was 1976, when dubious encounters were quaint adventures rather than mortal peril; so let the harmless fantasy come true for a night. Very little trouble yielded Nick's telephone number, and I made the call for Mac and set up an appointment. Nick sounded as one might have expected, trashy and agreeable. No, you wouldn't kick him out of bed—but you wouldn't want your brother to marry him. He wasn't in the least thrown to hear that his date couldn't talk.

"You should see some of the things I get with," he said. "Once I went to a meet and this guy had no legs." He laughed. "So whattaya think of that?"

Instinct warned me to arrange Mac's date for as soon as possible; I did not picture Nick keeping a terribly precise engagement book.

"How about now?" he asked.

It was a Saturday afternoon and Mac was game, so we cinched it—but it worried me that he didn't want me to stay and set things up with Nick, not to mention check him out for weapons. I never heard of Mac's taking an adventure alone. But he was adamant. "This fantasy I must not share," he wrote. The urgency was unnerving.

Worse yet, Mac refused to tell how the date had gone. That he had a wonderful time was unmissable; the grin was showing about twenty-five more teeth and the nod came a hair more slowly now, as if Mac had grown younger and wiser all at once. Bits of dish would slide out of him perchance; Nick had spent the weekend at Mac's that first time; Nick lived in a hole in darkest Brooklyn; Nick was seeing Mac regularly at bargain rates; Nick was very pleasant under the mean-streets facade.

Suddenly Nick moved in with Mac.

Dennis Savage, when he heard, was shocked silent for a good two minutes, an ideal condition for him. Our Mac—so he had become, for to befriend him was to own him—consorting with sex-show debris? When Dennis Savage regained his voice, he went into a ten-minute tirade reproaching me for encouraging Mac in this vile stunt, for having the sensitivity of Mickey Spillane, and for living. How was I to know that a date with a hustler would yield romance? Whoever heard of the fantasy coming true? I had always thought hustlers were the ultimate tricks, guaranteed for one time only, impersonal and beyond reach. Would not fantasy begin to dissolve at the touch of real life? Why else is "the morning after" as terrible a term in gay as "no exit" is in hell?

Yet Mac's fantasy held. I saw it in the way he spoke of Nick and to him—and Nick, fascinated by the gestures of hand and face that made words for the rest of us, would stare in smug wonder and cry, "Go for it, sport! Go for it!"

Mac did, all the way. It was dinners with Nick, cinema and hamburgers with Nick, Monopoly with Nick—the first American I've known, by the way, who couldn't play the game. You don't realize how broad our range of kind is here in the magic city till you meet someone who doesn't know what Monopoly is. I've played it with Ph.D.s and little kids, with the birthright wealthy and users of food stamps, with actors and construction workers, with competitors and nerds. Some mastered it—to the point that they virtually knew where they would land when they were shaking the dice—and some learned by playing, and some were frankly not apt. But everyone knew what it was. Nick had never heard of it—could not, moreover, pick it up no matter how carefully we explained it. My friend Carlo, who likes just about everyone and has a superb ability to forgive hot men their little misdemeanors, walked home with me after this Monopoly game and, in a lull, pensively regarded the traffic and said, "Tell me, who was that extremely terrible boy?"

Mac's coterie shook prickles at me for bringing Nick into his life, and, believe me, I did not rejoice. But the man was happy. No, he had always been happy; now he was cocky, getting around more by himself, doing what he wanted to on spunk, not on the assistance of his chorus of Rolfs. I found myself sounding, again and again, "I'm glad," for him. I hear tell of a chemistry bonding the socioeconomically energetic with the intellectually needy: yet what lies below Baltic Avenue?

[1985]

A STONE BOAT
Andrew Solomon

I DO NOT REMEMBER AT WHAT STAGE MY MOTHER ACCUSED ME OF giving her cancer. The episode was not so long ago; this forgetfulness is not like my inability to remember events of my early childhood. It's more that what she said was so sharp and so petrifying that it has frozen itself into words to which there is no chronology. I can remember a dozen subsequent related conversations, complete with their time and place. I can remember how, later, she apologized. That first conversation, though, eludes me. If I'm to be honest, I think part of the reason I cannot remember my mother's first accusing me is that she accused me only of what I already suspected to be true.

I can remember thinking when I was still quite young, and the idea of desiring men had all the terrifying resonance of novelty to it, that I could do nothing more terrible to my mother than to experience and act on those desires. "How could she have let you grow up thinking that?" asked Helen, later, but I don't know that my mother had chosen her horror any more than I had chosen my desires; and if her phobia was terrible for me, I accepted that it was probably no worse than my sexuality was for her. I can remember days when I had angered her, when she would complain at me in flushes of passionate rage—I can remember that this secret was my unacknowledged revenge on her. I would lie in the silence of my own room and imagine the pain I would later cause my mother, and I would exult in the appalling longings, in which, for all that I too hated them, there was power such as I had never before known. I believed at an early age that I could destroy her life; I had thought that I would use my desire someday to punish her. But I did not quite suppose that it could kill her. I thought of it as modern war-makers think of the most powerful weapons in their arsenals, as something too terrible to call forth, as something whose very existence could be the basis for an uneasy peace, as a device the precise effects of which were too complex and unspeakable to predict, too frightening even for secret tests on barren plains.

It was part of the love my mother and I had for each other to bruise each other, part of my love to plot injuries that, by and large, I did not inflict. But the most terrible injury of all, at the very prospect of which I had trembled, was one I could not help inflicting in the long run. By the time I talked about these matters to my mother, I wanted not to hurt her. I wanted somehow to take the unspeakable vengeance I had early recognized and make it sound like bliss, to show her a love as beguiling as my interpretations of Schubert. I wanted to be as perfect as one of my mother's holidays or parties, blighted by nothing more than the chance misfortunes of the weather, of a guest's cancelling at the last minute, of a slight argument among friends. If she could not see Bernard as an "A" on a report card in a key subject, I thought she might be able to see such love as a "B+," something far away from her, not quite what one might have wanted, perhaps, but really perfectly all right in the midst of all those other high grades and music prizes.

I could not—for many reasons—explain to her how much more effort, how much more battle and agony, had gone into what she saw as my great failure than had gone into the many things she saw as my successes, how much harder it was for me to live with Bernard than for me to play Liszt. My relationship with Bernard was a triumph. What might my mother have said to other tales, to the real narratives of loneliness that lay between those angry afternoons when I was fourteen and my discovery of Bernard when I was twenty-four? If I had really wanted vengeance on my mother—but by then, that was the last thing I wanted—I would have told her all the insipid and hackneyed details of one-night stands in which affection was less of a consideration than disease and the grim prospect of attack. I would have narrated the anonymous encounters with strangers in which there was no correlation between pleasure and joy. I would have spoken of meeting men of every class and proclivity, sometimes four or five in a single day, in locations as dangerous and ugly as the Ritz was beautiful, of occasionally being hit, of occasionally hitting someone back. I would have described hiding from the police when their approach had interrupted a fitful spasm in the arms of some aging and mild-mannered sadist in a public park, trembling half-naked behind a scruffy shrub and trying to be as still as in a childhood game of hide-and-seek. I would have told her how unthinkingly and casually I gave myself into the hands of unknown men, how I, though I disliked sharing a glass with a friend, would open my mouth to the chapped lips of a nameless unshaven figure in faded jeans and a torn T-shirt, and give up that self my mother thought she knew to his immoderate hands.

There were whole embarrassing catalogues, spectacular lists of tedious and uninventive humiliation that I could have provided. I had descended to a level of banality that was so shocking in itself as almost to outweigh, in my mind, the pain of experiences. If everything that has ever happened to me has happened in the same moment to my mother, then there can be no excuse for what I did to her in those years; the very thought of it all would have made her more violently sick than two years, than twenty years of chemotherapy.

But in fact, two things remained unsaid when she died, and this was one of them. Why should the tiresome matter of eros have been such an issue between us, when we were otherwise so linked? I blamed her for the ache of those sordid contacts that had stood in for adult love, as much as she blamed me for even imagining them. It ceased to be clear whose fault they were, even whose encounters they were. I have said that my mother never knew of them, but she knew me too well not to guess. I thought then and think now that she guessed everything. Since she thought my life was part of her life, my actions did not so much reflect badly on her as destroy the order she had selected and built for herself.

"And you're so unhappy yourself, Harry," she would say to me.

"Because of you," I protested. "If I didn't have to think the whole time about how unhappy my life makes you, I could have a jolly old time of it myself."

"There's no point blaming me," my mother said. "I'm sorry if I make things harder for you, Harry. I don't want to make things harder. I'm sorry that your life, as you now lead it, is not what I would prefer. But"— her voice took on an ironic tone—"you're a big boy now, and you make your own happiness or unhappiness. You have to take a little responsibility for yourself. You can spend your whole life blaming me because you're unhappy; you can tell the whole story to a psychoanalyst someday, and say how your impossible mother ruined your life. But that's not going to make you happier. By then you're going to be talking about a ruined life. Believe me—I want to see you happy, more than anything."

Bernard, whom I wanted so much to love, was caught in the middle of all this—he himself was in some ways of so little significance in my relation to him, except as a convenient line of demarcation, that it was often difficult, when I was in New York, for me to remember what he was like. I don't know how he put up with it.

The week my mother became ill, she said to me directly what had been implicit. She played the trump card that by some mutual agreement neither of us had ever played. She said, rationally enough, that her type of cancer was frequently brought on in women of her age by circumstances of stress. And she identified the primary source of stress in her life as my relationship with Bernard. And she finally said out and out what had always been hidden, what I had always feared might be true: that my desire was killing her and would kill her. For her to think as much was perhaps inevitable; we had set that up long before. But for her to say it was so terrible that I could not put it behind me, and will not.

[*1994*]

BASEBALL IN JULY
Patrick Hoctel

AT 30, I'D GOTTEN A BAD CASE OF BABY FEVER, AND IT HAD LASTED a whole year now. With that fever had come a bemused sense of betrayal. I'd been exhausting my disposable income sending baby gift after baby gift to various straight friends who'd claimed *they'd* never have children. Gay friends were having babies through artificial insemination or other means and talking constantly of parent networks and alliances between gay and lesbian households. Occasionally, my one-on-one relationship with Pim seemed distinctly passé.

Sitting there in my brother's den with the pink, gurgling Marie on my lap wasn't helping to reassure my biological clock. I was happy Pim was sleeping. He thought I got a bit silly when a baby was in the room. I wasn't gaga or anything, but I had to admit to a few kidnapping fantasies. Marie living with Pim and me, a dream nursery with a life-size giraffe and billowy curtains.

"He's a looker," Aunt Tee-Tee said, interrupting my baby reverie. "Not American."

Mother shifted her weight on the sofa beside me. "Danish," I said.

"I never heard him talk," she said, "so I didn't know where he was from. Of course, there aren't many men named 'Pim' in the state of Texas."

Aunt Tee-Tee had been watching us from behind the living room drapes. "His family came over when he was seven," I said. "He talks just like us. But no drawl."

"Where do you know him from?" she asked.

She meant how. How did I know that man down the hall? The blond in the bed. I glanced at my mother trying to seem so absorbed in her granddaughter. Maybe this one time doesn't count, I told myself. I'll probably never see Aunt Tee-Tee again and now mother is giving me a look like she's calling in her markers for the past 30 years. I was glad Pim was out of earshot, oblivious to all goings-on.

I heard Harvey Milk saying, "Come out, come out, come out!" But the picture in my head was of a scene 25 years before: I am sitting on the edge of a pool and an instructor is cajoling me to swim across its width. But I won't be moved. Not by sweetness—"You're such a good swimmer"—or threats—"You'll be the only one not to and you don't want that."

I was afraid of the deep water, having almost drowned the year before. First, I was scared, then mad at being singled out in the instructor's singsong voice. I didn't say anything. I didn't even look at the woman, but I knocked her hand off when she tried to grab my shoulder and pull me into the water. This was met with a chorus of disapproving clucks from the mothers on the other side of the pool, all gathered to see their children perform. I was the finale, but I wouldn't budge. My brother came over and squatted beside me. He whispered that Mom had said to do it. I caught her dark green lenses in their silver frames fastened on me. She wasn't smiling, only waiting. Neither one of us moved.

"We own a house together," I said. Mother looked pained.

"It's a *great* house," Larry said, coming to my rescue before Tee-Tee could jump in. "Overlooks downtown, and from the other side you get a view of the Bay Bridge. Pre-earthquake, 1885. Hardwood floors, fireplace in the main bedroom, and one in the living room. All the amenities."

Aunt Tee-Tee was momentarily overwhelmed, and before she could collect herself after Larry's onslaught, Marie cut her off. "She's wet or worse," Mother said.

"Fillin' her drawers," Tee-Tee said. "How I remember that!"

"I'll take her," I said. Marie was proving to be more valuable than I'd thought, although I hoped she was only wet. Mom got up with me, both of us seizing the excuse to absent ourselves.

"Don't help him, Janet," Tee-Tee said, her voice tracking us down the hall to Marie's room. "He'd better start learnin' to do that himself."

"I *know* how to change a diaper," I said, more to myself than to Mom or Marie. "I worked in a daycare center for a year and a half."

"Theresa means well," Mother said. "And she doesn't know about your string of odd jobs."

Mom was moving in on Marie's bassinet, handling the whole procedure herself. The only sounds in the room were the baby kicking and my mother's breathing, heavy from bending over the child. I didn't feel like getting into my work record, why it was how it was, so I let it go. Instead I made Marie's mobile jump up and down for her, butterflies scattering to the left and right.

"I don't know why you had to say that to her, anyway," Mom said. She dropped the filthy diaper into a hamper. "There are other things you could've said."

"There's a limit," I said.

"You could've said you're friends or you're co-workers. I don't see why it's necessary for Theresa to know that you live in the same house."

"Right," I said. "A co-worker is going to travel with me from California to Texas for my niece's christening. That makes sense." Mother was giving Marie's bottom lots of powder; clouds of talcum were settling over the baby. "You're going to choke her," I said.

"Your Aunt Tee-Tee means well," Mother repeated. "But she talks too much. I don't know what she'll say or to whom. She comes out with anything that strikes her."

"So what," I said. This was old ground for my mother and me. "Tee-Tee lives in Houston. You don't know anyone in Houston."

Mom scooped Marie off the bassinet. "I'm 65," she said. "I don't need any more upsets. People used to care what other people said of them," Mother added. "About their reputations."

I wanted to shout, but I knew this would bring Tee-Tee on the run. "It's your reputation," I said. "That's what this is about."

Mother patted Marie's back, trying to raise a burp. In the fading afternoon light as she lay Marie in the crib, I was startled to see her hair, although jet black on top, was now a dreary shade of white at the roots. "I don't gray pretty," she'd once said.

"You don't understand," Mom said, straightening up. "People can be nasty. You haven't learned that. Maybe your ways are fine for California, but here they'll smile and nod their heads—and then do something awful. I don't want you hurt."

Mother bent down to fuss over Marie and turned her back on me in such a way as to indicate that our talk had ended. I didn't mind, though. I wasn't thinking about our talk. I was thinking about how close we'd been when there was that lie of omission between us and now how she was once again the woman in the silver-frame glasses on the other side of the pool, waiting for me to swim across.

[1988]

FAG HAG

Robert Rodi

FINALLY, NATALIE BELIEVED IT. SHE BELIEVED THAT LLOYD WAS A threat, the worst ever.

She didn't go home that night; she crawled into Peter's bed and lay there, empty of feeling. Still no anger. She wondered where it could be. Didn't she love him? Then why didn't she feel the violent rage she always felt when someone new came into his life?

She wondered about it for hours, her head on his pillow, her eyes wide. Eventually she determined a reason: She couldn't feel anger because, unlike Peter's other lovers, Lloyd hadn't taken Peter away—instead, he had changed him utterly. The Peter she loved wasn't involved with a new man; the Peter she loved did not exist at the moment. He'd been battered into a new shape by Lloyd's constant hammering.

She fell asleep wondering how she could bring him back again. It was so important that she bring him back again. She might have no clear idea of the life she wanted to lead with him, but life without him was inconceivable— a vast expanse of misery, stretching on until her death. And if a romance with Peter sometimes seemed just as inconceivable, well—tough. She was going for broke. It was either the peak, the summit, the acme—meaning Peter—or nothing. Whatever kind of love they could share—even the flimsiest, the least satisfying—even if she had to utterly debase and humiliate herself to get it, that's what she wanted. He was her highest value, the full realization of her image of perfect humanity, perfect masculinity.

Except for that one little area, of course. That one little, damnable, excruciating, unshakable area.

At the crack of dawn, she got up, dressed, and left Peter's apartment, not wanting to be there when he arrived to change for work.

A few hours later, he phoned her from his office. "Lloyd and I made love last night." That was how he put it. Not "Lloyd and I slept together" or "Lloyd and I had sex." It jolted her. She'd never heard him speak of "making love" to anyone.

"It was—it was—well, words fail me." Words have never failed him before. "It was like the fulfillment of something I didn't even know I'd been dreaming of." He'd never spoken of fulfillment before. He'd never spoken of dreams before. "Such incredible intimacy. Such a powerful sense of, I guess I'd call it rightness." He'd never spoken of those things before. "I'm in love with him." He'd said that before, but now his tone was that of a different man.

"Oh," she said, her voice dead of expression. "Congratulations."

"I told Lloyd that you were with me when I played his messages. I told him that you were as moved by it as I was, that it actually made you cry. He was really touched by that; he hadn't realized how close we are. He wants to have you over. To his place, for dinner, just the three of us. He says he's a good cook. Guess we'll find out together. Friday okay?"

"Okay," she said.

"You sound funny. You all right?"

"Fine," she said. "You'd better get back to work."

"I know. Well—thanks for listening, doll. I love you."

"You're welcome."

She hung up.

Still no anger. She felt dead of all feeling. Where was it hiding?

She walked through her week like a zombie. She smiled at no one. On Wednesday, the head of the office where she was working called her agency and asked them not to send her back; she'd given the other employees "the creeps."

She ate lightly all week. She hadn't any hunger. Nothing so strong as an appetite or a desire in her. Her meals were joyless. Her sleep was dreamless. She watched television without laughing. She listened to music without pleasure.

On Thursday night, she found her anger.

She was at the Evergreen supermarket, picking up a few staples. Milk, bread, nothing colorful or exciting. She didn't check the prices; she didn't care. She would pay whatever the clerk told her she owed. Nothing mattered.

She heard someone call her name. "Natalie!" It was Peter's voice.

She turned. It had sounded as though he'd been directly behind her, but she didn't see him there.

"Hey! *Natalie!*"

Wait—*that* was him. The man she'd looked right past.

He came up to her and kissed her; she stared at him in horror. She thought she might be sick.

His hair was gone. He'd gotten a haircut. There was almost nothing left. Nothing to shake the water out of, nothing to let blow in the wind, nothing to tousle, nothing for her to run her fingers through. He'd gotten a haircut.

He noticed her shocked expression and self-consciously ran his hand over his scalp. "Oh, you noticed, huh? It was supposed to be a surprise when you came to dinner tomorrow night. I know, I know—it's a little more boot camp than I wanted, but it'll grow. Lloyd likes it this way."

"Th—that's why you did it?" she said, her voice shrill. "For *Lloyd?*"

"Well, mostly. He didn't like the long-hair look. Tell you the truth, I was getting a little tired of it myself."

She was trembling. Tears popped out of her eyes. "My God—I'm really losing you, aren't I?" she said.

He grimaced. "Oh, come on. It's just a haircut."

She shook her head. "It's more than that. You're gone, totally gone. Everything I once—" Her voice was in danger of breaking; she forced herself to stop. "Peter, you have to excuse me. I can't talk right now. I'm too upset."

"I don't understand you," he said, annoyed. "Why does everything have to be so fucking dramatic?"

She felt like the earth was moving. "Excuse me," she said. She left her cartful of groceries and walked out of the store. She went directly home and crawled into her bed. A few minutes later, her doorbell sounded. Peter no doubt. She ignored the insistent ringing and eventually it ceased.

She quaked with anger. Her bed shook. Her teeth gritted against each other. An hour passed. Two. Her telephone rang and she wouldn't answer it. Soon the sun disappeared and she lay in darkness, clutching her pillow. She looked balefully out her window at the starless sky. Her bed shook.

[1992]

SECRET LIVES

Francis King

WHEN OSAMU ARRIVED THAT AFTERNOON, THE ROOM WAS EMPTY. For a terrible moment he thought that, in his absence, Brian must have died. Then the familiar sight of the flotsam of haphazard objects which invariably gets washed up around a patient—the open copy of Ruth Rendell's latest novel, lying face down on the bed, the unopened box of Charbonnel and Walker chocolates, brought days before by Jeremy and Lucy, on the bedside table, the crumpled ball of a handkerchief on the floor, where it must have fallen—reassured him. They must have taken Brian off for one of those treatments or tests which he still, to Osamu's amazement, consented to endure.

Osamu sat down on the cold, slithery edge of the one armchair in the room, head on one side as though listening to some far-off sound, gripped his clasped hands between his knees. He felt tired both from despair and anxiety and from the ferocious cleaning which he had given to the Highgate house in an attempt to convince himself that, in a day or two, Brian would return to it, as he kept insisting that he would.

The door suddenly opened. Osamu and Andy stared at each other.

Then Osamu jumped to his feet.

"Have I made a mistake? Have I come to the wrong room?" But as he asked the questions, Andy saw the Ruth Rendell novel on the bed before him. It was he who had brought it for Brian the day before. "I was looking for Sir Brian Cobean."

"This is his room. But he is not here. I think that maybe . . . a test . . ."

Osamu had never seen Andy; Andy had never heard of Osamu, much less seen him. Yet each was later to think, with bewildered wonder: Somehow it was as though I had known him for years and years.

Andy now walked into the room, his thumbs stuck into the pockets of his tweed jacket and his head high.

"You're waiting." A statement, not a question.

Osamu nodded. Then he made a gesture towards the armchair, as though he were pushing something invisible with the palm of his hand. "Please."

Without a word, Andy perched himself on the bed. He picked up the novel and stared down at the pages at which it had lain open. He felt his heart racing unpleasantly—tachycardia, Bragg had called it, when he had consulted him about it, nothing serious, probably due to the strain of poor old Brian's illness. He drew one deep breath and then another. He coughed.

"You're a friend of Brian's?"

"Yes, I am his friend."

"And you are from . . . ?"

"Japan."

"I've never been to Japan. The nearest I ever got was when I put in a spell of duty in Hong Kong. I recently met the Japanese ambassador at a dinner party."

"I do not know Japanese ambassador. I regret."

"Did you and Brian meet each other when he went there on that case?"

"Case? No. We met in London. In Holland Park."

Andy got up from the bed and crossed to the window. He looked out through the double glazing at the traffic speeding over the Thames. He turned. "Where do you live?"

"I live in Highgate. I live in Brian's house."

The two men stared at each other.

"But I've never met you there. Brian never told me . . . I imagined . . ."

Osamu shook his head. He said nothing.

"Have you know each other a long time?"

Osamu again said nothing. Head now tilted sideways on its long neck, he was gazing at the radiator.

At that moment Brian, supported by one of the Sisters, returned to the room.

"Father! I thought you said you wouldn't be coming until this evening..."

"That was the idea. But then I was asked to make up a four at bridge and so... Have I done the wrong thing?" He looked over at Osamu.

"No, of course not!" With a small groan, Brian eased his emaciated body first on the edge of the bed and then across it. "Thank you Aileen," he said to the nurse.

"Can I get you anything?" She had been slapping the pillows as though she wished to hurt them.

"Nothing, thank you."

The nurse went.

"You two have never met. Osamu, this is my father." He left the introductions at that, putting his head back on the pillows and closing his eyes.

"I guess that it is your father."

Eyes still closed, Brian said: "Ossie—would you mind? There are things my father and I must talk about... Could you wait for, well, half an hour?"

"I can wait."

Osamu got to his feet, walked over to the door, turned as though he were about to say something, and then left.

Andy was often to wonder why he had never then questioned Brian about the Japanese, as he was also often to wonder why Brian had never made any attempt to explain him.

"How are you, old boy?"

"Oh, a bit better, I think. What's the latest on the Parkinson front?"

"Well, you won't believe this. Last Friday he actually had the cheek to ask me for a rise..."

It was, in essence, a conversation which they had had each time that Andy had made a visit to the hospital.

[*1991*]

ROSEN'S SON

Joe Pintauro

Setting:

An apartment foyer on the Upper West Side
of Manhattan, New York City.

Characters:

MR. ROSEN is about sixty.
EDDIE is forty.
HARRISON is twenty-eight.

*Two men, one old enough to be the father of the other, are sitting on
the floor of an apartment foyer. The older man is lying with his head in
the lap of the younger, like a child who has been crying. There is quiet
in the foyer, although we are aware that something awful has just
happened, something that caused the men to collapse to the floor. The
older man is still in his wet raincoat; his umbrella is on its side next to
him, dripping on the floor tiles. The younger man, who apparently
just answered his buzzer, obviously had been entertaining dinner guests.
He is dressed handsomely for dinner. Perhaps some coats, hats, and
umbrellas of guests are hanging in the small foyer. Doors to the foyer,
imaginary or not, are closed, one supposedly locked.*

MR. ROSEN: Forgive me, Eddie.

EDDIE: Shhhhh.

MR. ROSEN: Do ya forgive me?

EDDIE: I think so.

MR. ROSEN: Where's the gun?

EDDIE: I've got it.

MR. ROSEN: Did I hurt you?

EDDIE: My lip's cut.

MR. ROSEN: I'm sorry.

EDDIE: Just take it easy. Relax.

MR. ROSEN: I've gone crazy. I miss my boy.

EDDIE: I miss him too, Mr. Rosen.

MR. ROSEN: So you get involved two months after he dies?

EDDIE: Your son was sick a long time.

MR. ROSEN: So you celebrate his death by moving a stranger in here to live with you?

EDDIE: He's no stranger.

MR. ROSEN: You call me "Mr. Rosen"?

EDDIE: All right. Ziggie. Take it easy.

MR. ROSEN: Strangers' coats in my son's foyer.

EDDIE: Just shut up.

HARRISON (*Off.*): Ed?

EDDIE: Yeah?

HARRISON (*Off.*): Who buzzed?

EDDIE: I'm taking care of it.

HARRISON (*Enters, speaking*): Our guests are waiting. . . . Who is this man?

EDDIE: Ben's father. (*To Mr. Rosen*) This is Harrison.

HARRISON: Mr. Rosen?

MR. ROSEN: What else?

HARRISON: My deepest sympathies . . . for your recent trouble. Would you care to join us? (*He indicates the dining room.*)

EDDIE: No, Harrison . . .

MR. ROSEN: I come here with a gun, he invites me to dinner?

HARRISON: Does he have a *gun?*

EDDIE: I took it from him.

MR. ROSEN: Does he know who allows him to stand here in this foyer? My son. Because of his death you stand here. Is that true Eddie? I would vomit on that table in there.

HARRISON: He's off his rocker. . . .

EDDIE: This is not him.

MR. ROSEN: Young people, you have no hearts, no memory, but wait. You'll get yours. Just let me outta this death oven.

EDDIE: I'll call you later.

MR. ROSEN: Call nothing. Which way out of this hell?

EDDIE (*Grabbing his coat, to Harrison.*): I've got to go with him.

HARRISON: You're *going?*

EDDIE: To see him home.

MR. ROSEN: Are you crazy? For me what is home?

HARRISON: Eddie, you can't just leave our dinner guests.

EDDIE: Shut up, will you, Harrison?

HARRISON: Are you aware of the tone you just used with me?

EDDIE: *I said shut up.*

HARRISON: I'm calling the police. He's threatened us.

EDDIE: Do that, Harrison, and I'll leave you. I swear to Christ.

HARRISON: Did you say you'll leave me?

MR. ROSEN: Easy come, easy go.

HARRISON (*Pointing at Rosen.*): You are trespassing, and it's criminal.

MR. ROSEN: Bite your tongue, cutie. Who do you think you are to get your bloomers in such an uproar over me? What do you see standing before you? An old man in a raincoat. One wife. One child. Both dead. Him I put in the diamond business. For you, bastard.

HARRISON: Does he mean me?

MR. ROSEN: Who do I mean, this umbrella? You start living with a man two months after his lover dies—are you the Blessed Virgin?

HARRISON: I knew Eddie a year.

MR. ROSEN: While my son was sick you fooled around, you pig in a fancy shirt.

EDDIE: He worked in our office.

HARRISON: You're wrong, Mr. Rosen.

MR. ROSEN: Drop in a hole the two of you. Young people. You replace other people like spark plugs. Half your age I said good-byes that would make you sweat blood. I cut the tattooed numbers off my wrist with a kitchen knife, then worried, without them, how would my sister find me. Don't worry. Your government brought the numbers back worse and you got them and no knife is sharp enough. . . . You. I tried to teach you, but only diamonds you learned, only money so you could marry Mister Bloomingdales here who tells me I trespass in my son's apartment? *Mazel tov.* Give me at least back my gun.

HARRISON: Don't give it to him.

EDDIE: Get inside, Harrison.

MR. ROSEN: Afraid to die so young, Mister Bloomingdales? My boy was not afraid. He smiled. Relax, Mister Bloomingdales, the gun was for my head not yours or his, though you are pigs enough to be slaughtered. . . .

EDDIE: Ziggie, please.

MR. ROSEN: Shame on people who eat with candles, not for God but to hide pimples and wrinkles. Young people who live together not for love but for sex, boff boff like pistons machines. You never get bored?

(*To Harrison.*) What are you smiling at?

EDDIE: Harrison, go now. (*Harrison starts off.*)

MR. ROSEN: Not so fast, cutie. You wanna make a deal? You change places?

HARRISON: With who?

MR. ROSEN: My boy?

HARRISON: Oh, Eddie.

MR. ROSEN: You crawl into his grave and send my son home to his father?

HARRISON: I'm so sorry for you, Mr. Rosen. . . .

EDDIE: Harrison's a good person.

MR. ROSEN: Young people living in a magazine. Did you show him a picture of my boy? (*Mr. Rosen takes out his wallet.*)

EDDIE: Jesus!

HARRISON: I'm not afraid. I'd like to see him.

MR. ROSEN (*Showing him the photo.*): Look at a beautiful face, Eh?

HARRISON: Very nice.

MR. ROSEN: You . . . (*To Eddie.*) What's his name?

EDDIE and HARRISON: Harrison.

MR. ROSEN (*To Eddie.*): *Goyisha?* (*Eddie nods yes.*) Harrison. Where do they get these names?

HARRISON: It's a family name.

MR. ROSEN: Your nose is a fortune cookie next to my son. I'm serious.

EDDIE: Okay, Ziggie, let's call it quits.

MR. ROSEN: A basketball is your neck. My way of speaking. You play an instrument?

HARRISON: I've always regretted not . . .

MR. ROSEN: The flute, my son . . . Avery Fisher Hall. Clippings to drown in.

HARRISON: He's extraordinary. He's beautiful. (*Handing back the photo.*) Eddie, our guests are waiting.

MR. ROSEN: I came here to splash my brains over your table. That's what the gun was for, to put out your candles with my blood.

HARRISON: Please.

MR. ROSEN: But I changed my mind. In the river throw the gun. Me, I'll do like the elephants: Go to Miami. The sun will polish my bones. For a little fee, a lawyer will send you my tusks. They'll be nice here, either side of your door. Speaking of doors, kindly point the way a person gets out of here.

HARRISON: May I be excused please?

MR. ROSEN: Leave. *Mazel tov.* (*Harrison exits. Rosen stares long at Eddie.*) You forgot the summers at the lake, the canoe, the three of us? The dinners? The holidays, birthdays? I had to accept you, didn't I? I had to swallow it. And I did. And you just forgot those days?

EDDIE: I didn't forget any of it.

MR. ROSEN: Were we really together then?

EDDIE: I thought we were.

MR. ROSEN: I thought so, too. I thought so. (*Eddie puts on his coat.*) Where you goin'?

EDDIE: To help you get a taxi.

MR. ROSEN: No taxi.

EDDIE: Then I'll call you later to see you got home safe.

MR. ROSEN: Never dare call me again in your life. You're nothing to me.

EDDIE: Don't say that.

MR. ROSEN: Liar. You want I should disappear so bad.

EDDIE: No.

MR. ROSEN: Look at his face. Such a liar. After this minute, never, never again will you see this face of your "*Mr. Rosen.*" But before I go I want you should tell me a truth, so perfect as you never before spoke the truth to anyone in your life, and I'll give you the freedom of a thousand doves set loose on the mountaintops.

EDDIE: Ask me.

MR. ROSEN: Do you love that one in there? The truth before God.

EDDIE: I'm trying to love him. I'm the kind of man who has to have somebody.... I'm trying very hard. (*Rosen moves in on Eddie, beating him down with questions.*)

MR. ROSEN: Does he take care of you like—?

EDDIE: He's different. . . .

MR. ROSEN: Like my boy used to? Remember—

EDDIE: Different.

MR. ROSEN: Like you were God on Earth?

EDDIE: No.

MR. ROSEN: Does he laugh with those same funny eyes. . . .

EDDIE: Of course not.

MR. ROSEN: Bake bread like he used to?

EDDIE: No. (*Losing it.*)

MR. ROSEN: Play the flute on Sunday while you read the paper?

EDDIE: No.

MR. ROSEN: The truth before God.

EDDIE (*Shouts.*): *It'll never be the same for me again. Never.*

MR. ROSEN: This is true?

EDDIE: What do you think? (*Eddie falls, crouches at Rosen's feet, weeping.*) You bastard, you awful man.

MR. ROSEN: Good you cry. Now I'm happy. Good-bye, Eddie. Don't follow me. Don't call me. God bless you. You were my son. Really. You were. My other son. (*Mr. Rosen exits, lights fade on Eddie.*)

[*1989*]

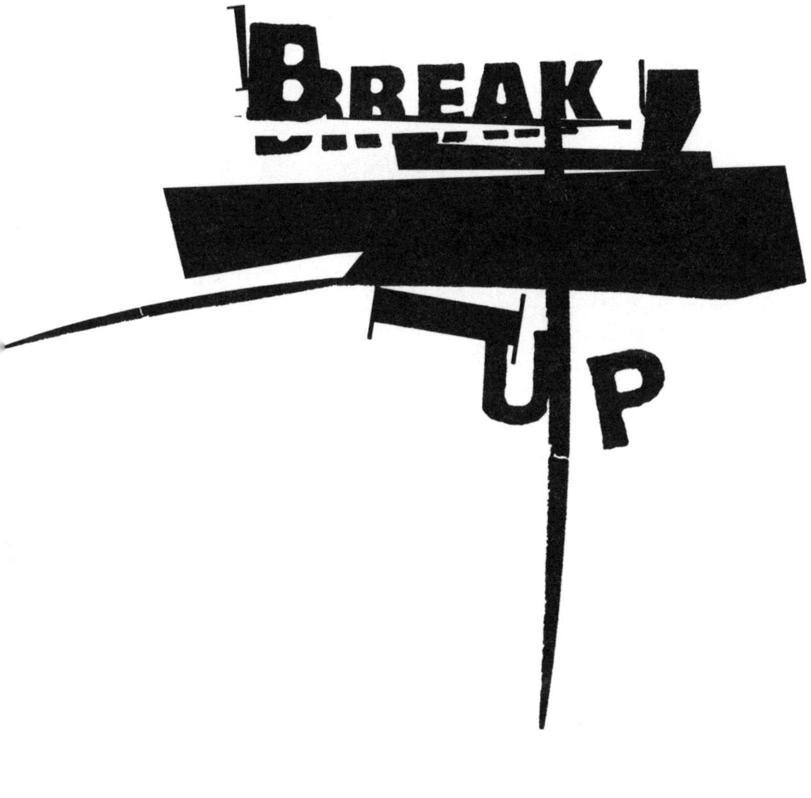
BREAK
UP

FURTHER TALES OF THE CITY

Armistead Maupin

THE BAND WAS PLAYING "STAND BY YOUR MAN." AS SOON AS THEY recognized the tune, Michael and Ned smiled in unison. "Jon was big on that one," said Michael. "Just as a song, though. Not as a way of life."

Ned took a swig of the Calistoga. "I thought it was you that left him."

"Well, *technically*, maybe. We left each other, actually. It was a big relief to both of us. We were damn lucky, really. Sometimes it's not that easy to pull out of an S & M relationship."

"Wait a minute. Since when were you guys...?"

"S & M," Michael repeated. "Streisand and Midler. He was into Streisand. I was into Midler. It was pure, unadulterated hell."

Ned laughed. "I guess I bit on that one."

"I'm serious," said Michael. "We fought about it all the time. One Sunday afternoon when Jon was listening to "Evergreen" for about the three millionth time, I suddenly found myself asking him what exactly he saw in...I believe I referred to her as 'that tone-deaf, big-nosed bitch.'"

"Jesus. What did he say?"

"He was quite adult about it, actually. He pointed out calmly that Bette's nose is bigger than Barbra's. I almost brained him with his god-damned Baccarat paperweight."

This time Ned guffawed, a sound that told Michael he had struck pay-dirt. Ned was the only person he knew who actually guffawed. "It's the truth," grinned Michael. "Every single word of it."

"Yeah," said Ned, "but people don't really break up over stuff like that."

"Well . . ." Michael thought for a moment. "I guess we just made each other do things we didn't want to do. He made me alphabetize the classical albums by composer. I made him eat crunchy peanut butter instead of plain. He made me sleep in a room with eggplant walls. I made him eat off Fiesta Ware. We didn't agree on much of anything, come to think of it, except Al Parker and Rocky Road ice cream."

"You ever mess around?"

"You betcha. None o' that nasty heterosexual role-playing for *us*. Lots of buddy nights at the baths. I can't even count the number of times I rolled over in bed and told some hot stranger: 'You'd like my lover.'"

"What about rematches?"

"Once," said Michael grimly, "but never again. Jon sulked for a week. I saw his point, actually: once is recreation; twice is courtship. You learn these nifty little nuances when you're married. That's why I'm not married anymore."

"But you could be, huh?"

Michael shook his head. "Not now. Not for a while. I don't know. . . maybe never. It's a knack, isn't it? Some of us just don't have the knack."

"You gotta want it bad," said Ned.

"Then, maybe I don't want it bad enough. That's a possibility. That's a distinct possibility." Michael took a sip of the mineral water, then drummed his fingers on the bar in time to the music. The band had stopped playing now; someone at the jukebox had paid Hank Williams Jr. to sing "Women I Never Had."

Michael handed the Calistoga back to Ned. "Remember Mona?" he asked.

Ned nodded. "Your old roommate."

"Yeah. Well, Mona used to say that she could get by just fine without a lover as long as she had five good friends. That about sums it up for me right now."

"I hope I'm one of 'em," said Ned.

Michael's brow wrinkled while he counted hastily on his fingers. "Jesus," he said at last. "I think you're three of them."

[1982]

THE BOLD SAILOR
Stan Leventhal

EVER SINCE WAYNE LEFT, I HAVE KEPT MYSELF SO BUSY THAT TIME
is something that is no longer part of my conscious thought. I cannot
gauge or measure it and have lost the ability to control it. I seem to exist
apart from—above or below, I'm not certain which—the rush of time.
Haven't escaped it. I can feel myself aging. Slowly. But still, somehow, I
am removed.

On the third day of Wayne's search for employment, I returned home
and found him cursing the heat and concrete sidewalks.

"What's the matter?"

"I called my sister to wire me some money 'cause it looks like I might
not find a job as fast as I thought. Anyway, she told me that Mom is in
the hospital."

"Is it serious?"

"Brain tumor."

"Oh, my God!" I hugged him and comforted him as best I could.

"I'm gonna catch the 9:47 bus."

"Is there anything I can do? Do you feel like eating something?" He
nodded. I glanced at the clock.

"Just enough time to get some groceries. After we eat, I'll help you
pack and we'll go to the station together. All right?"

When I returned from the supermarket, however, he was gone. He'd
packed his belongings and left the keys in the mailbox. I could not find a
note with a telephone number where he could be reached.

The next day, I received a call from the employment agency. Wayne had been accepted for the position of clerk at a "chic private hotel." I said I'd have him call as soon as I heard from him.

I went about my work absentmindedly for several weeks, wondering what was going on. Eventually I received my phone bill, which registered a long distance call to somewhere in Massachusetts, "between Boston and the Cape," as Wayne had once said. I walked around for a few days with the bill in my pocket, anxious to call, afraid of what I'd find out.

Late at night, a few days later, I dialed. His sister answered. He wasn't there, nor did she know where he was stationed. I introduced myself, and she said that Wayne had spoken of me. "As long as I have you on the phone," I said, dying of curiosity but fearful that I was intruding, "I'd just like to find out how your mother is doing."

"What do you mean? She's fine, as far as I know."

"I see. That's a relief."

"Did Wayne tell you she was sick or something?"

"In a word, yes."

"Oh, honey, that's just Wayne's way. He's been making up stuff like that ever since he was a kid."

A few days later, I received a hastily scribbled note from Wayne in which he apologized for having lied about his mother's health. He went on to explain that he was afraid he'd never find a job and would not allow himself to be supported by another.

I didn't really speak to anyone for weeks. When friends would call, I'd say that I was busy and would get back to them when I was able.

I'm desperate to let him know that he was accepted for a job, but he's always drunk when he calls, and he never lets me know where he is so that I can write him. Although he stays in touch, communication is impossible.

All I have now is work, time, and memories, which function together like an automated Mobius strip. And I still have the records he gave me. There's one song in particular that constantly runs through my mind. It's about a bold sailor who leaves his lover to go to sea, each one keeping half of a broken coin. Years later, when they meet, they do not recognize each other at first, but the parts of the coin match perfectly, and they realize that they have been reunited. Sometimes I have a dream that is like a surreal film of that song with Wayne and myself as the main characters, mandolins and concertinas snaking across the soundtrack. Only when we meet again, we recognize each other instantly. The two halves of the coin, however, do not fit.

[1 9 8 8]

LIFE DRAWING

Michael Grumley

IT WAS LATE WHEN I FINALLY PULLED AWAY FROM LEOPOLD AND OUT of his sticky lair, so late the stars were out and the moon was filling up with light and the night birds were busy in the trees. It might be James was still asleep and I could keep mum; maybe you did something like this and just walked away from it. Dad had once said that a man has to take his actions upon himself, and keep them to himself—that telling all and whining for forgiveness only put the burden on somebody else. Was that true?

Back at Mrs Odum's the supper plates were still clean on the table in the dining room, and the sound of Thomas watching TV in the kitchen seemed to me reassuring, calming. I crept up the stairs, but caught the glances of Mr Mulkin and Mr McBride, who were sitting in the parlor playing checkers. I felt they could see everywhere my body had been and everything it had done in the last few hours. But they were gentlemen, and seeing me creeping in so furtively, pretended they didn't see me at all.

Upstairs, the light was off in James's room, and that was when I should have left well enough alone. But I was in a state, and had to be sure everything was as it was before my adventure—that was a good word for it— and so I pushed his door open and peeked inside.

"Mickey? I been wondering where you all got off to. Come over here. Come on. . . ." He was propped up in bed, with no light but the moonlight coming through the window, and I couldn't tell how long he'd been awake.

In that light, there was something catlike about his eyes, the deep brown shining with a milky blue. I came to him and lay down beside him.

"I'm sorry I've been outside so long. Just drawing, out in the park, trying to get something done...."

He didn't say anything in reply, and I pressed close against him. He'd thrown off the sheet and lay smooth and naked in the patch of moonlight, and I thought, This is a painting, this is art, just this.

In a soft voice he asked, "Where's your drawing pad?" His hands weren't moving on my body the way they usually did; he was waiting, hanging in the moonlight.

I'd left my pad at Leopold's. Thrown in the chair with his old lady's dress patterns. Left behind, forgotten.

"Gotta get a new one," I said, in my squeaky little voice. "Used it all up."

"I bet you did," he said, slow and deliberate. He sat up, facing away from me on the other side of the bed. "Better take a shower," he said in a flat voice I'd never heard before, " 'cause you be smelling like something out of a whorehouse."

He was up and pulling on his slacks and shirt, bending over to lace up his suede shoes.

"James..." I didn't know what words would come out of my mouth, but the panic I felt was something I had to cover over.

"I don't want to hear it. Whatever you think you gotta say, you go tell it to the wall."

He was standing by the door now, and I jumped out of bed and tried to put my arms around him, but he pulled away. And I guess he saw in my face the fear and panic and shame, and maybe he relented a little; for a minute, he let me hold on to him.

Then he was out the door and down the stairs. And I wasn't half of something glorious anymore; I wasn't sure and proud and invincible—I was shivering and cold in an overheated room in New Orleans, somebody small and insignificant and alone, somebody who's just thrown away more than he knew he had.

[1991]

 *David Sedaris*

THE PRESS IS HAVING A FIELD DAY OVER THE NEWS OF MY relationship with Mike Tyson. We tried to keep it a secret, but for Mike and me there can be no privacy. Number one, we're good copy; and number two, we just look so damned good together, so perfect, that everyone wants pictures.

Charlton Heston and I are finished, and he's hurt. I can understand that, but to tell you the truth, I can't feel sorry for him. He had started getting on my nerves a long time ago, before the *People* story, before our television special, even before that March of Dimes telethon. Charlton can be manipulative and possessive. It seems to have taken me a long time to realize that all along I was in love with the *old* Charlton Heston, the one who stood before the Primate Court of Justice in *Planet of the Apes*. The one who had his loincloth stripped off by Dr. Zaus and who stood there naked but unafraid. What a terrific ass Charlton Heston used to have, but, like everything else about him, it's nothing like it used to be.

In the papers Charlton is whining about our relationship and how I've hurt him. I'm afraid that unless Charlton learns to keep his mouth shut, he's going to learn the true meaning of the word *hurt*. Mike is very angry at Charlton right now—very, very angry.

Let me say for the record that Mike Tyson, although he showers me with gifts, is *not* paying for my company. I resent the rumors to the contrary. Mike and I are both wealthy, popular men. The public loves us and we love one another. I don't need Mike Tyson's money any more than he needs mine. This is a difficult concept for a lot of people to grasp, people who are perhaps envious of what Mike and I share. This was the case with Charlton Heston, who lost most of his money in a series of bad investments. It's sad. The man is a big star who makes a fortune delivering the Ten Commandments one day, and then loses it all as a silent partner in a Sambo's restaurant chain the next.

Mike and I would gladly give everything we've got in exchange for a little privacy. We would be happy living in a tent, cooking franks over an open fire on the plot of land we bought just outside Reno. Mike Tyson and I are that much in love. It is unfortunate that our celebrity status does not allow us to celebrate that love in public. Since we were spotted holding hands at a Lakers game, all hell has broken loose, and the "just good friends" line has stopped working. None of this is helping Mike's divorce case or my breakup with Charlton, who, I might add, is demanding some kind of a settlement. For the time being, Mike Tyson and I are lying low. It's killing us, but we've had to put our relationship on the back burner.

[1994]

THE CATHOLIC

David Plante

AS WE DROVE INTO BACK BAY, OUR TALK ABOUT THE NUDE KEPT OPEN
the promised sex between us. But Henry could see the nude denuded of
sex, as, say, an object of history. He was deeply interested in history
(I wasn't really) and he talked mostly of poems, plays, novels from the
point of view of the periods in which they were written (I regarded them as
transcending all periods). I couldn't deny that his approach was probably
better, because less sentimental, as a valid appreciation of literature; my
approach left literature inexplicable, which was not an intelligent appreciation, but an ecstatic one. With him, I was absolutely sure that my approach
was wrong and implied defective intelligence, while his approach, filled
with intelligence, was right. But while I admired him, I wished he were able
to detach himself, just a little, from his sense of serious study, which was,
to him, work, and take me up for trying to be funny about it—especially
now, when I wanted to bring it all down from the sky into our laps, to
resolve it into fucking. But maybe Henry was ashamed to talk about sex.

Then I thought: he doesn't allow himself to say anything, to do anything, that is in any way self-conscious.

I reached out and grabbed his thigh and squeezed it, digging my fingers
into it.

"Be careful," he said quietly, "or we'll have an accident."

I took my hand away.

Everything is going to be all right, I said to myself, you'll see, everything is going to be fine.

I let my body go loose, tilted my head back, and closed my eyes. My skin was tingling with sunburn and dried sea salt. If, for now, I couldn't touch him because it was dangerous, I could, in anticipation of touching him later, touch myself, and I slipped my hand under my tee-shirt.

You'll get everything you want, I thought.

Then this event took place: I felt myself thrown off-center and pulled to the side, and when I opened my eyes, I saw the maple trees along the street, lawns, porches all pass as the car, with a long screech, swung round. I went rigid, and even when the car stopped, facing the opposite way, I felt some continuing momentum would make the car inevitably crash, and I waited for the impact. I knew what it would be like. I felt that it was about to occur, and I reached out to hold Henry. My arms went round the motionless body leaning slumped against the steering wheel. Henry's eyes were open and staring.

I tried to pull him towards me. He turned only his head to look at me, though he seemed, too, to look through me. I said, "Henry." He asked in a low voice, "Yes?" "Are you all right?" "Yes," he went on in the same low, still voice, "I'm all right." There was no traffic in the sunlit street. We sat for a while longer, then Henry turned around and continued.

In silence, we drove into Black Bay. Students were lounging on the stoops and stairs of the brownstone houses. Henry stopped in front of the house where I lived.

Before I could say anything, he said, "I've been thinking I should go back to my apartment and work."

"Right," I said. But I didn't move, half thinking: this isn't everything. I opened the car door. "Thanks," I said.

He nodded.

I got out of the car and held the door open, then shut it when he went into gear.

I was twenty-four years old and I had studied myself in different circumstances enough to recognize the outward signs of my reactions to happenings. On the sidewalk, I saw in the many details—a crack in the cement, a popsicle stick—that what was happening inside me had happened before. I didn't want it to happen again. The details held me for a while. I shook my head and looked into the distance, where the heavy sunlight blurred. Then I went up to my room. I stared at the map of Boston tacked to a wall.

What happened? I asked myself.

Look, I told myself sternly, whatever happened was entirely to do with him and had nothing to do with you. You said nothing, did nothing to make him leave you standing alone on the sidewalk the way he did. Nothing. And yet I kept asking myself, What happened?

Put it out of your mind, I thought. Without too much difficulty, you can put it out of your mind. Put what? Never mind what. Just stop thinking about it. About what? Stop it, now. Stop it? Yes, now.

[1985]

A DIFFERENT PERSON

James Merrill

CLAUDE HAD ME TO LUNCH. IT WAS A LOVELY SPRING DAY. HIS FRENCH windows, open onto tiny balconies, overlooked the Piazza di Spagna six flights below. Quinta presided in a cheerfully visible kitchen—how unlike mine—and the round table had been set for three. Above it hung a mobile of wire and wooden balls, vaguely planetary, a new addition. I'd seen his apartment just once before but felt greeted by things I recognized, above all by the serenity they achieved under his roof, which my own unruly belongings could never aspire to. The books stood in thoughtful order, a little Murano vase I'd given him held a fresh flower, the Olivetti slept like a parrot beneath its patterned kerchief next to the densely typed pages of Claude's vast, ongoing journal. Over a glass of wine we talked of Ravenna. Out came a book on the mosaics I might like to borrow. Alice had written; she was well and said I owed her a letter. They were doing *I Puritani* next month at the opera—had I ever heard it? I understood: he was treating me as a guest. I glanced again at the third table setting and waited for the doorbell to ring. Or did the new person already have his own key?

"It's gone on ten months," Claude was saying in his difficult murmur, but with a merry twinkle. "We've agreed that the end's in sight."

What had I missed? It was unlike him to talk so openly of a failed romance, but I supposed he had Dr Detre to thank for this new, rather callous frankness. Ten months? So the affair had begun while we were still together, soon after our move to Rome. Feeling wronged in retrospect, I asked—since I had to say something—if "he" was Italian.

Claude stared. "I don't understand."

"Your friend of these last ten months...?"

"I was talking about my analysis, about Tom," said Claude, still puzzled. (He called Dr Detre Tom, just as he used *tu*, like a true Italian, when speaking to Quinta—with whom I had locked myself into the formal *Lei*.) "The year he'd originally estimated is nearly up. I forgot an appointment the other day. It's a classic sign that the patient is ready to move on. But you thought—" As the nature and implications of my mistake dawned on him, Claude broke into uneasy laughter. The doorbell rang.

Quinta admitted a frail, black-haired young man, who greeted her familiarly. Claude introduced him as Jorge, an artist from Peru. His was the assemblage of hoops and spheres that hung above us as we sat down to lunch. At once I liked it less. I found Jorge plain, his deferential manners at odds with my latest notion of table-talk on a sunny day. Of course he and Claude were lovers; the lunch had been arranged to make this clear. Was he the "best Claude could do" in Rome? It pleased my vanity to think so, and to remind itself that Robert would soon be returning; the part of me that wished Claude well was depressed.

Not that I was entitled to show any of this. Love had once allowed us to read each other in the dark. Now the psychic lens opening had contracted; we must let what could be made out by friendship's plain daylight guide us, without reference to that secret nocturnal terrain we no longer stumbled through. Here a more exciting thought broke in. If Dr Detre was planning to send Claude home—cured!—in six or eight more weeks, wouldn't my own term end shortly thereafter? I decided not to ask the doctor this question; it would have been like glancing at one's watch during the salad course. Nor did I intend to bring up my impressions of Jorge lest, like Montale, he dissolve on closer inspection into Dr Detre himself. Whose precise, amused voice I could hear already: "...this yellow-faced foreigner Claude has been seeing secretively, who has replaced you at the center of his life." I didn't need to be told by my shrink that I'd been chafing under his schedule. After Ravenna, I wanted to visit new places by myself and taste the drug of solitude in each of them. And for the first time in months, at the risk of sapping the creative energy I was expected to bring to our analytical work, I found myself fiddling with a poem. It began with some negatives of photographs I'd taken of Robert and ended by returning him—or "her," as convention dictated—to the status of a perfect stranger:

> Here where no image sinks to truth
> And the black sun kindles planets in noon air
>
> The lover leads a form eclipsed, opaque,
> Past a smoked-glass parterre
> Towards the first ghostliness he guessed in her...

Quinta's *risotto primavera* was delicious. I mentioned my forthcoming weekend in Cortona. ("It is now officially spring," Umberto had said in his deep drone, "and the rooms are no longer freezing.") "You will be near Arezzo," said Jorge, "where the great Piero della Francesca frescos are. Have you ever seen them? For me he is the supreme Italian painter." I had not; I knew Piero's works chiefly from photographs. Marilyn had visited the famous *Flagellation*—"In Urbino," said Jorge reverently, and began to enumerate the other Pieros, peasant madonnas and farmboy saints, rendered with a dispassion itself amounting to saintliness, which studded central Italy like solitary gems, while Claude gazed fondly at him, pleased that our talk was giving his friend a chance to shine. Although these things were worth hearing, Jorge's account of them struck me as wooden and impersonal. What, I wondered not without slyness, was the best book on Piero? The dim young man named it eagerly; it was the source of his passion; no more than I had he stood before the paintings themselves. Claude's eyes now met mine in a brief, intensely neutral look. "You and I may feel," the look said, "that it is pitiful to boast of second-hand knowledge; nevertheless Innocence is as precious as Experience, and I will thank you not to snub my friend." I felt the justice of a reprimand that must have been made more than once on my behalf, when Claude was my lover and I rattled mindlessly or tipsily on. So the luncheon party left a sour aftertaste.

[1993]

THE HEART HAS ITS REASONS

Felice Picano

Not because you didn't call.
I almost half expected that.

Not because we set a date
you just couldn't make—
whatever your reasons.

Not because you never arrived,
never left a number to reach you.
For all I know you were hit by a car;
mowed down in some neighborhood war.

Not because the night I had planned
never got off the ground
never mind reach the heights.
We didn't have that much in common
except a good fit—
if you still can remember that fondly, that far.

No, not because you stopped a trip
never gave me the chance to decide
whether or not I'd take the ride,
whether I'd take the risk of true love or illusion.

But simply because
I straightened all day.
Washed all the glasses
changed pillows and sheets
cleaned out the closets
even laundered the drapes.
Did everything that was needed
if a guest like you was coming.

Did, in short, what could wait,
For that I could never forgive you.

[1983]

THE ORTON DIARIES

Joe Orton

FRIDAY 24 MARCH

Day began sunny. Went for a walk. Caught a bus back at Euston. Kenneth is off to hang his collage-pictures at Freddie Bartman's antique shop, Anno Domini, this afternoon. At two Freddie rang and said he hadn't any nails. Kenneth found that we had some in a tin. He went down to Chelsea by tube at half-past two. The pictures, about twenty in all, we framed a while ago.

After Kenneth had gone I cleaned the bathroom. Then I had a glass of milk and went down the Holloway Road in search of a bit of sex. It was a grey day. The wind blew dust in everybody's eyes. I went round a back street near the tube station and into a lavatory. Only a fattish man in a blue woolly. I wasn't particularly interested. Several more men drifted in: all ugly. In the end the place was full and I decided to leave. I passed through the place, looking to see if any were worth having and suddenly noticed that one—a youngish man—wasn't bad. He followed me out and we walked under the bridge. He was Irish. He had a pale face, hollow cheeks, but pleasant. I said, "Have you got anywhere to go?" "I share a room with a mate," he said. I thought this meant that he had nowhere to go. So I said, "I don't know anywhere round here." "D'you like three-somes?" the young man said. I shrugged. "It depends who the other fellow is," I said, thinking at the time that this was a very sensible remark because his mate might be hideous. "You can come back with me," he said, "if you like." "Won't your mate mind?" I said. "I wouldn't be taking you back if he did, would I?" he said, which was another sensible remark to put with mine.

His name was Allan Tills. He was a security guard. I thought he meant police at first, but this wasn't the case. His mate worked in a bar. They had a flat in Highbury. The flat was in a big Victorian house painted blue, and in good condition. His mate was in when we got to the door. I went for a piss and when I came back his mate was introduced to me as Dave. I realised at once that luck was with me: he was well-worth the effort. He had pale blue eyes and had a day's growth of beard. He wore jeans and a check shirt, under the shirt a white vest. He was about twenty-five years old and came from Burnley in Lancashire. He had a softness about his body which wasn't the softness of a woman. I hoped he would let me fuck him. I didn't anticipate having to persuade him. "D'you want anything to eat?" he said. I said I didn't. "We're going to have a meal." A. Tills said, "I'm famished." We went into a kitchen. They got fish and chips for themselves and I had a cup of tea. "Where d'you work?" blue-eyed Dave said. "At the British Drug Houses," I said, thinking that it would be ridiculous in a situation like this to tell the truth. "Where d'you come from?" he said, a bit later. "Leicester," I said. "I've got a mate who plays for Leicester City," he said. "I slept with him on the night before his wedding." "You must've ruined his wedding night," I said, more for want of something to say, since the remark hardly made sense. "Yer," Dave said.

We went into the bedroom after this. It was a large room with a print of ships in a harbour on the wall. There were two beds—a double one and a single one. On the single bed was a lot of clothes. "For the laundry," A. Tills said. He came round and kissed me. "D'you mind threesomes?" he said, in a rather prurient way I thought. "No," I said. He got undressed. He had a thin body, a fuzz of black hair on his chest, a large cock. I didn't take my pants off immediately. Neither did Dave. I remembered that in Tangier Marzuk wouldn't either. In the bed everything went remarkably well. I necked with A. Tills more to show willing than anything else since I'd much rather have begun on Dave. It was like having to eat bread before touching the jelly at school parties. After a decent interval I turned and necked the blue-eyed Dave who had a very sexual body. A. Tills sucked my cock. After a while I turned Dave over and shoved my cock up his arse. He gave a yelp and I took it down. A. Tills produced vaseline and I put it on my cock. A. Tills put some up the blue-eyed Dave's bum and I began again. It went up like a treat. "Flat! Lie flat!" I said. He did so. Whilst I fucked his arse, A. Tills pulled himself off. Also, and I remember thinking, "Kinky Irish Catholic get," he kept smacking my buttocks. Actually it was quite exciting. After I'd come and withdrawn, I noticed A. Tills had come. Dave rolled on top of me and rubbed himself off on my belly. We lay in bed for a while, half-asleep. The ceiling was v. clean. Moulding of leaves. An alarm clock beside the bed said 4:00. "I must go at five," I said, thinking that Kenneth would be back by then.

A. Tills became amorous again in about fifteen minutes. I got the horn. But didn't really want to be bothered doing much. I got on top of him and began necking him. He moaned a lot. Then, rather to my surprise, the blue-eyed Dave, also with his second wind, began to push his prick up my arse. It seemed rude to refuse to let him do to me what I'd already done to him. And so I let him fuck me. Whether he came or not I don't know. A. Tills said afterwards he felt crushed flat. "Come again sometime," Dave said, switching on the television set which burst into life with *Winnie-the-Pooh* by A. A. Milne[1]. "We'd love to have you." I did take the address. Whether I'll call again is another matter. "The best night for us is Monday or Wednesday," A. Tills said, as he let me out of the front door. I thought they were both very nice fellows.

[*1967*]

---

1. A. A. Milne (1882–1956). Prolific author of plays, novels, biography and essays, all over-shadowed by his children's books. *Winnie-the-Pooh* (1926).

FAST-FOOD SEX

Andrew Holleran

MOST DINNER PARTIES HAVE TWO LIVES: THE DINNER ITSELF, AT which you gather with others, and the remembered dinner, which is far more delicious, actually. Just as Wordsworth savored the beauty of his jocund daffodils while lying at home afterward in a reverie, so a dinner party fulfills itself as a recollection, when the dish on the table gives way to the dish on the telephone. I just learned, for example, that a recent visitor from San Francisco—a cherubic journalist—told our host at a dinner we attended together that he found the other guests cerebral, New Yorkish, and antisexual. He got this impression when someone remarked that he'd had sex only three times in the past year and I said, "How civilized, how discreet!"—half ironic, half in earnest. The San Franciscan thought I was completely serious, and it confirmed his worst suspicions. "You look so weary, all of you in New York," he told our host the next morning. "Well," said the host sweetly, "that's because we *are* weary."

Weary of sex even—yes, I'm not afraid to admit it: I *was* congratulating that man for having sex only three times in the past year. The last time I had been intrigued by a sexual confession (such a staple in gay life, one would almost prefer a companion discuss nuclear fission) was when a friend told me of a fellow he had had to date nineteen times before he could kiss him. How marvelous that in 1979 someone would still refuse his person to another! For people aren't refusing their persons much any more. In fact, grabbing a body is about as easy as going downstairs and buying a hamburger—which is why in San Francisco they call it "fast-food sex."

When I first arrived in New York, friends would walk past buildings and say, "Oh, that was the Triangle, that was the Stud, that was...," and I'd listen to tales of back-room bars as exotic as palaces of the Ming dynasty. In those days you would be ejected for blowing someone in a certain bar, but history has come round. Now that bar sports closed-circuit TVs on which pornographic films unfold; slides of Colt models appear on another wall, and the live men at your side have sex right there. The city has more baths and discotheques than ever before, and more homosexuals to have sex with. Visiting Sheridan Square has become an almost frightening experience: they come down Christopher Street like an army, in ranks and ranks, and (here's the nightmare) all of them are hand-some, all of them your physical ideal. It's the doom of Don Juan: must I go to bed with *all* of them? A friend looking at this homogeneous mob one Sunday afternoon moaned, "It's like an invasion of the body snatchers."

And that's just what we all want, isn't it, kiddo: to snatch a body, to use someone's genitals and get off on his smooth, flat stomach.

I was delighted later to run into the man my friend had dated nineteen times before kissing. I was crossing Washington Square on a snowy Friday dusk, and he was out walking his dog. A handsome man in a gray topcoat whose collie was romping with some other dogs around a tree, he seemed embarrassed when I introduced myself and said how rare a species I considered him.

"It's not what I want, believe me," he said, blushing slightly. "But yes, it's true. In the old days I loved the very things I loathe today—like that fellow there" (he nodded at a young man crossing the square in torn jeans, engineer boots, hooded sweatshirt, and leather jacket). "Five years ago, the gayer the outfit the better. Someone like that struck me as a soldier of sex—devoted, in uniform, solely at the service of the only thing I lived for, sex with another man. Now" (the young man was disappearing into the trees) "I look at him and think: how ghastly, to extinguish one's individuality, to dress as a human dildo.... Everything that attracted me five years ago now seems totally stupid. Getting blown is so easy now, and so meaningless, that it's about as significant an event as a sneeze!" He turned to watch his collie hurl itself against an imperturbable Great Dane, then continued.

"My friend says that men are like dogs, they should screw every day, but," he sighed, "I'm afraid I've lost that talent. Last week in the baths I was sitting in a corner waiting for Mister Right when I saw two men go into an even darker nook and run through the entire gamut of sexual acts. And when they were finished—after all these *kisses*" (he was suddenly agitated) "and *moans* and *gasps*, things that caused scandals in the nineteenth century, toppled families, drove Anna Karenina to suicide—" (he raised his eyebrows) "after all that, they each went to a separate bedroom to wash up. Now, you may view this as the glory of the zipless fuck, but I found it suddenly—and it surprised me, for I'd always adored this event before—the most reductive, barren version of sex a man could devise. Barbarella was more human pressing her fingertips against the angel!"

"Fast-food sex," I said.

"Fast-food, twentieth-century, American sex!" he said, his face excited in the soft light of the descending sun.

"Well," I said, half ironic, half in earnest (that New York vice), "we've destroyed many aspects of the previous century, you know: luxury liners, formality, long lunches, handmade lace, leisure, and court balls. I guess we'll destroy sex, too."

"We already have! My orgasms don't interest me any more! Why do these assholes praise promiscuous sex, say there's nothing wrong with it, that because we're gay we're leaders in a brave new world who will set new patterns of behavior, and all that crap, when even sex, on that basis, ceases to be erotic? Do they really think that because we're gay, young, and urban we don't have the same need for fidelity and intimacy that any other human beings do? When sex is as easy to get as a burger at McDonald's, it ain't too mysterious or marvelous, believe me."

"Oh, I'm sorry," he said, lowering his eyes and then raising them to fix me with a desperate stare, "but you can't imagine how awful it is. To be gay, yet no longer able to respond to other gay men because you know it will only be an exchange as profound as eating an Egg McMuffin—I feel as if I've developed a disease or something, and I'm doomed to wander as a ghost, alienated from my own kind."

A man in a blue wool hat sauntered up to us: "Loose joynts, man, Valium, methadone, Black Beauties, anything that turns you on."

"Go fuck yourself," muttered the man my friend had dated nineteen times, and he began to walk westward with his dog. "I'm in a terrible mood lately," he said, "because I'm just as lonely as ever, and just as horny too, and yet I won't, I can't do it just for sex any more, it has to be with some kind of interest in the human personality connected to the genital," and he gave a deprecating little laugh.

[1983]

THE LEATHER BAR

Ralph Pomeroy

Tonight, at the bar,
in the Members Only room,
the usual collection of aging 'cyclists'
lounge
wearing painfully tight jeans
elaborately arranged to show
maximum amount of cock and balls.
Even in summer a lot of them wear full leather.

Some are young—too young to be so pale,
so negative looking—and wear
that stupid expression resorted to
by those who try to appear indifferent.
They congratulate one another on some
new refinement in their get-ups—
a line of studs outlining their pockets,
a cleverly blocked cowboy hat, a pair
of real German Army boots.

Amid the greetings and badinage
a pool game goes: focus point—
because of the brilliant light bouncing
off its green field—
for involved nonchalance, exhibitions of
strained, tattooed muscles, 'baskets,'
arching asses.

Cracks are made about someone wearing
mere shoes or—God forbid!—sneakers!
These are The Boys, The Fellas, The Guys.
So, if someone ambiguous enters, sunny
from a lucky weekend, rested from enough sleep,
not drinking at the moment, in a good mood
really—
and is dressed for the heat
in an old open-necked shirt, loose pants
and sandals—
they look up, stir uneasily.

To them, he doesn't project a butch enough image.
The masses of long golden hair don't help.
His smoking a small, delicious cigar is a
gesture too filled with the 'wrong' style.
Immediate alienation.

But those who know him,
those who have been to bed with him,
know what they know.
He exchanges greetings with them—
of varying degrees of warmth.
And the sly, furtive, taken gazes
will pass back and forth all night
through the dark smoke.

Sizing up. Sizing up. A puzzle pieced
together: 'If A's been to bed with C and
seems to like him, and I've been to bed
with C and we got on fine, then maybe A
would work out for me...
And he knows G whom I've always wanted
to make-out with... He could tell me
what G digs... Guess I better move
over to a better spot so I'll be more
directly in his line of vision...'

The clock, which advertises beer,
says half-past two. Tomorrow's a working day.
Yet the bar stays full with a Great Number
yelling from the juke box.
No one wants the night to end yet.
Most hope to connect with someone—
impersonally, in a group, or maybe
personally,
one at a time.

[1983]

TWO BARTENDERS,
A BUTCHER AND ME
Daniel Curzon

I'D JUST GOT OVER A BAD CASE OF MENINGITIS, COMPLICATED BY MY diabetes, and my doctor had told me the day before that I was probably getting kidney stones too. (Nobody knows what pain is until he has had kidney stones, believe me.) So when the guy from San Francisco stared at me in the bar and then came over and asked if I wanted to join in an orgy, you can understand why I felt good. I realized I must look a bit puny with my thin shoulders and thinner arms, my fat lips and dwindling hair (though I'd cut it flat to make it look less obvious). But the guy from San Francisco was making the overture, saying he and his lover, Gil, were arranging an orgy. They'd already asked the bartender if he wanted to have a four-way, and the bartender had said he did. I guess they liked my face. It turned out that Gil was a bartender too—up in San Francisco, not here in Fresno—and for a minute all four of us sort of eyed each other, seeing how we felt about getting together.

To be honest, the Fresno bartender, Rory, didn't turn me on very much. He was cute and growing a nice beard, but somehow he seemed a little silly. (I'd seen him running around the bar lots of times before, but we'd never spoken.) Gil was pretty good-looking. Far better than me in fact, with elegant gestures and a deep voice. The best of the lot was the guy from San Francisco, a butcher, who was slim and solid and lots of fun. Up close, he looked a little dissipated, because of the dark marks under his eyes. That night he'd had about six White Russians and had been smoking grass and even sniffed some amyl out on the dance floor, so I wondered if I would be getting in over my head by getting into an orgy with those guys. But the guy from San Francisco, Bill, was really full of life and having a great time running back and forth between the three of us, finding out who liked to do what.

I began to get sleepy before the bar closed and thought of leaving, since I had to get up and go to work at the Welfare Department in the morning at eight. But somehow or other I hung in there. I was going to lose my job anyway in a couple of months, because the budget had been cut, but I didn't want to lose it for coming in worn-out from an all-night orgy. Still, I kept asking myself how many offers for an orgy at the Fresno Holiday Inn did I get in a year, anyway.

So I waited around while the two guys from San Francisco danced and the bartender closed up. I was getting a little worried because I don't have a very big dick and Bill talked about cock a lot, as though size was very important to him. I didn't want him to be disappointed when I pulled my pants off. (I know it's not supposed to matter if you have a little dick, but it does, it sure does.) I tried looking over at Rory, but he didn't catch my eye, and I figured he wasn't attracted to me any more than I was to him. But I also figured a three-and-a-half-way was better than a no-way, so I hung in there.

Somehow some Italian guy got involved. He was supposed to make up the fifth in the orgy, but when we left the bar I found out, in the parking lot, that Rory had lost interest in the Italian and didn't want him to follow us in our cars out to the Holiday Inn. I felt sorry for the Italian because he didn't catch the hint and followed us all anyway, and then, at the motel, Rory had to lie and say that all of us were acting "so weird" that he didn't plan to stay. So the Italian guy was left out in the cold. I guess he went on home.

The other four of us went into the motel room and took our clothes off. There was a big tray of dirty dishes and half-eaten food on one of the double beds, and the beds were unmade and clothes were thrown everywhere. It was all a little messy, but I suppose you wouldn't want an orgy to be middle-class and super-clean anyway, right?

I didn't know exactly what I was supposed to do, but the butcher gave me a sniff of amyl and asked me to fuck him while Rory was fucking him too. It was pretty wild, I guess. It was the first time I'd ever seen a guy get fucked with two cocks at the same time—and I was one of the guys doing it! I kept thinking about the Italian who'd been invited and then not invited, wondering if he was still in the parking lot, sitting in his car by himself. Of course, I hadn't said anything to the others about asking the Italian to join us, so I guess I made him feel not wanted, too.

So we all fucked each other in various combinations, though Rory and I didn't touch very much, just a little bit near the end. And nobody said anything about my little dick, though I think Bill was maybe a little disappointed. But if I have to defend myself, he couldn't have been fucked by me and somebody else at the same time if we'd both had big ones.

When I got off, I was sitting on Gil's dick, and the other two were watching from the other bed, even encouraging me to come. I suppose if anybody had been watching from a peephole it would've seemed nasty or depraved or something, but it didn't seem like that from my angle. We even joked around a lot and hugged and told each other we were good sex. We got so loud that Bill shushed us and said we'd wake up his mother. I thought he was kidding, but it turned out he wasn't. His mother really was in the next room. She was traveling with them, and she knew about him and Gil and took it all with a grain of salt, though she wouldn't talk about it.

The moment I remember the most is when Rory, who was really quite a good fucker, was giving it to Bill, who had his legs up in the air and was grunting. Gil and I were resting on the rug and Gil says to me, quietly, "I really love him. I love him so much." He meant it, too, and I thought that was sort of nice. Here he was watching some bartender from Fresno fucking his lover in the ass and he was glad because it gave his lover pleasure.

About four-thirty I slipped out and left the other three sleeping. Didn't get a chance to say goodbye. I got to work on time (still have a month to go on my job and I can get unemployment for a while after that).

For some reason that evening didn't seem funny or depraved or anything. All I know is that when I was sucking dick and getting fucked and fucking that night, I didn't feel like I was a skinny thirty-eight-year-old with a little dick that nobody wanted. Of course I knew that nobody there in the Holiday Inn "loved" me, but for a while I felt that life wasn't passing me by, and I guess I'm kind of wishing some guy from San Francisco would come on through Fresno some other night, maybe soon. It wasn't perfect, no, but it was *something*. Maybe it was even sort of sad if you think about it too much, but then aren't most things in life sad?

[*1981*]

JEFFREY

Paul Rudnick

(*Jeffrey climbs out of bed. Lights go down on the bed and everyone in it. Jeffrey steps forward and begins to get dressed. He speaks to the audience.*)

JEFFREY: Okay. Confession time. You know those articles, the ones all those right wingers use? The ones that talk about gay men who've had over five thousand sexual partners? Well, compared to me, they're shut-ins. Wallflowers. But I'm not promiscuous. That is such an ugly word. I'm cheap. I *love* sex. I don't know how else to say it. I always have—I always thought that sex was the reason to grow up. I couldn't wait! I didn't! I mean—sex! It's just one of the truly great ideas. I mean, the fact that our bodies have this built-in capacity for joy—it just makes me love God. Yes!

But I want to be politically correct about this. I know it's wrong to say that all gay men are obsessed with sex. Because that's not true. All *human beings* are obsessed with sex. All gay men are obsessed with opera. And it's not the same thing. Because you can have good sex.

Except—what's going on? I mean, you saw. Things are just—not what they should be. Sex is too sacred to be treated this way. Sex wasn't meant to be safe, or negotiated, or fatal. But you know what really did it? This guy. I'm in bed with him, and he starts crying. And he says, "I'm sorry, it's just—this used to be so much fun."

So. Enough. Facts of life. No more sex. Not for me. Done!

And you know what? It's going to be fine. Because I am a naturally cheerful person. And I will find a substitute for sex. Sex Lite. Sex Helper. I Can't Believe It's Not Sex. I will find a great new way to live, and a way to be happy. So—no more. The sexual revolution is over! England won. No sex! No sex. I'm ready! I'm willing! Let's go!

[1994]

CRUISE CONTROL

John Edward Harris

UNION SQUARE

"You can't tell me that between 1970 and 1980 you slept with over a thousand men—it doesn't compute."

"Take three a week..."

"You had slow weeks, right? I mean, this is ten years."

"Three's average. Rounded down. Three times fifty-two times ten equals 1,560. Even if you say 2.5..."

Bob sucked and fucked his way through the seventies. I know that. I held my own through the eighties, treating my tubes as if they were like the temple of an unusually reticent god who feared human contact. I was content, secure in my belief that sex without commitment was self-destructive. As much as I would like to think that a decade of promiscuity destroyed his soul, I'm stuck with the facts: Bob's the happiest man I know.

"Oof. Did you see that?" Bob asks.

"What?"

"The messenger."

"Where?"

"On the ten-speed."

Bob points him out and I have to admit it's a nice ass, but that's not enough.

"The way he bounces on that seat you'd think it's a—"

"Don't say it."

"Dildo."

"This isn't a conversation, it's a hand job."

Bob and I met at the office, in the elevator. He said something inane about how humid it was; I said, "Sure hope it doesn't get as hot as last summer," and headed for the R train at 14th Street. When I realized that's where he was going, I decided to walk. Bob asked if he could join me. Given my midwestern manners, how could I say no?

Now I get a daily sermon on the mount—on how to mount—from the would-be savior of my sex life; I tell him to shut the fuck up, that it's the nineties and nothing's safe and nobody's free.

[1994]

LETTER FROM LYTTON STRACHEY
TO DORA CARRINGTON, 10 JUNE 1930

I HAD A CURIOUS ADVENTURE AT THE NATIONAL GALLERY WHERE I
went to see the Duveen Room—a decidedly twilight effect: but spacing
out the Italian pictures produces on the whole a fair effect. There was a
black-haired tart marching round in india-rubber boots, and longing to
be picked up. We both lingered in the strangest manner in front of the
various masterpieces—wandering from room to room. Then on looking
round I perceived a more attractive tart—fair-haired this time—bright
yellow and thick hair—a pink face—and plenty of vitality. So I transferred
my attentions, and began to move in his direction when on looking more
closely I observed that it was the Prince of Wales—no doubt at all—
a Custodian bowing and scraping, and Philip Sassoon also in attendance. I
then became terrified that the latter would see me, and insist on performing
an introduction, so I fled—perhaps foolishly—perhaps it might have been
the beginning of a really entertaining affair. And by that time the poor
black-haired tart had disappeared. Perhaps he was the ex-king of Portugal.

HOW TO CRUISE THE MET:
IT'S NOT JUST FOR OPERA ANYMORE
T.R. Witomski

A FEW WEEKS AGO A FRIEND WAS GIVING ME ONE OF THE TWICE-weekly installments of his *Tales of Woe* (which, now that I think of it, resemble a version of *Dynasty* in which all the roles are played by Joan Collins) when he launched into one of his favorite recurring motifs: the shortage of gay men in the Americas. Though empirically absurd, this topic is nevertheless one of the most dominant (and most submissive) themes in gay history. A typical expression of it goes something like: "It's impossible to meet people. I'm not really looking for a lover, but I'd like to meet *someone*. Forget the bars. After twenty years in the bars—did I say twenty?—I meant ten—I'm *over* alcoholics, clique queens, and writers, present company excepted. And now that we're not allowed to go to the baths anymore without being made to feel like Typhoid Mary, what's left? Don't suggest the personal ads—I still blame you, T.R., for the '30ish hunky adventurer' who turned out to be a sixty-two-year-old, three-hundred-pound Mafia hit-man who answered to the name of Baby Death. I'm too old to cruise the streets, too broke to afford a gay, gay, gay vacation, and everybody else at work is more fucked up than I am. There must be someplace to go to meet intelligent, employed, nice gay men."

Sure there is. It's called the Metropolitan Opera House and on any given night (except Sundays) from September to April, the place is loaded with faggots. Even if only 10% of the Met's audience is actively gay, at least another 10% is passively gay, and then there are those gays who can't make up their minds, those supermarket queens, the A/Ps. Anyway, the Met's a big place, so however you figure things like this (is a bisexual counted as being half-gay or three-quarters queer?), it's fairly safe to assume that there are a lot of gays at the Met. Even dismissing those gays who are ineligible due to prior commitments, offensive shoes, and incorrect opinions of Ghena Dimitrova, an evening at the Met will still place you in close proximity to *tons* of gays ready, willing, and able to make your bed more crowded. And a faggot you encounter at the Met isn't likely to be a mere dicklicker. Met gays tend to be college-educated, self-supporting, and well-behaved, smart, relatively affluent, nice dicklickers. Most Met queens could wear signs: "I can be taken to meet your mother without causing undue *tsuris* in Poughkeepsie."

Opera queens have gotten a bad press. They are thought to be cruelly bitchy, horrendously petty, and extraordinarily demanding. And they *are*. But at the same time they aren't the sort who'll throw up on you at bars, think Monsterrat Caballé is something you order in a French restaurant, or insist that they move in with you immediately after—or even during—the first fuck. Opera queens are probably the closest approximations to responsible adults one is likely to encounter in one's journey through gay life.

The negative image of the opera queen is largely due to the negative image of opera. Opera is thought to be a lot of fat people wandering around bizarre locales singing in foreign languages for many tedious hours. And it *is*. But, then again, a gay bar is a lot of drunk people wandering around bizarre locales either saying nothing or speaking in tongues for many tedious hours so it's not like going to the opera for the first time will be an entirely brand new experience for the typical cocksucker. Going to the opera is really very much like going to a gay bar (alcohol is available at the Met for those gays who are constitutionally unable to cruise without clutching a drink), only at the opera you can sit down for long stretches of time and even nod off without being thought a party pooper. (Best time for naps: the second act of *Aida*, all of *Francesca da Rimini* except the intermissions, whenever Venus is off-stage in *Tannhaeuser*, and during arias sung by Renata Scotto.)

If you are going to start cruising the Met (and you really should—

you owe it to yourself and the Met needs the money: Hildegard Behrens doesn't come cheap, no matter what she looks like), there are a few things you should know:

A) Forget old movies that show operagoers dressed in tuxedos and evening gowns. Despite whatever urges you have to wear an evening gown—and no matter how elegantly simple the dress—remember that except for the Met's opening night (which is terrible for cruising anyway), formal attire is only worn by tourists (i.e., people who read the libretto during the performance; it's okay, however, to follow the score—but learning to read music seems a very high price to pay when all you're essentially after is a wee bit of culture and a big dick). Reverse-chic is very trendy. You should try to look like you see going to an opera as a come-as-you-are party, something you just sort of show up for without paying it much thought. (Placido Domingo does this all the time when he's *in* the opera being performed, not merely *at* it.) Leather is permitted, sometimes even encouraged, and, occasionally, such as at performances of *Die Walküre*, demanded.

B) It is helpful to learn a few technical words that will enable you to converse fluently with opera queens. Now, watch my lips: "Of course, if you're the sort of person who likes that type of soprano (so-*pran*-o). . . ."
"Marvelous voice, but you know she's a lesbian (*lez*-bi-an), don't you?"
"If he can get through this role, I'm Marie of Rumania (Roo-*ma*-ni-a)"
"How about stopping for a drink at my apartment (a-*part*-ment)?"

C) Cruising the Met is a team, not an individual, sport. Though there is no law that says you can't go solo to the opera, a man alone at the opera is usually perceived to be a weird heterosexual. Lord knows you have enough problems without getting a reputation for *that*. (To answer your obvious question—Christ, I have to tell you fairies *everything*, don't I?: you start an opera team by having a few friends read this essay. No, Mary, you *don't* show them your copy; you send each selected sister out to buy his very own copy. An excessive pass-on rate doesn't mean shit when we come right down to the central reason for my telling you all this neat stuff: getting me more money based on increased sales of *Kvetch* by addressing the issue most readers are most concerned about—getting laid more.) Where was I? Oh yes, opera queens are pack animals, but mating is never done within the pack. The way it works: someone in your own pack knows someone in another pack, everybody gets introduced to everybody else, pair bonds are formed, and people marry and die without ever learning the plot of *Il Trovatore*.

D) Since the most successful cruising is done during intermissions (the Met is famous for long intermissions, often longer than the performance itself—*they know*), never, ever, attend an opera that doesn't have an intermission. *Elektra* and *Wozzeck* are cute enough, but hopeless for cruising.

E) When in doubt, criticize. Ignorance of opera is no excuse for holding your tongue. Even if you think High C is a fruit drink, don't know the difference between Tosca and Wotan, and couldn't hum "La donna e mobile" if your life depended on it, you can still be an opera critic: pick on the sets, the costumes, and the physical appearances of the singers (how fat is she?); knowingly intone "Well, she *has* been better"; kvetch about other audience members—"Yes, darlings, all through Isolde's Narration and Curse, this woman in front of me was chewing gum— what will the peasants do next?" When all else fails, lament the passing of Maria Callas.

F) Opera queens are very receptive to newcomers in their midst and eager to share their knowledge of opera, but don't needlessly annoy them. After witnessing two hundred-plus performances of *Carmen*, you won't be in much of a mood to have your mind fucked with either. Some things *not* to say:

At *Madame Butterfly*—"Funny, she doesn't look Japanese."

At *Tristan und Isolde*—"Isn't he *ever* going to die?"

At *Der Rosenkavalier*—"What is this? A dyke opera?"

At just about anything: "Since you know she's going to kill herself at the end, why don't we skip the last act and go fuck?"

G) Some operas attract more gays than others. Operas in German, operas longer than four hours, operas featuring famous fading divas are big favorites. Put these criteria all together and they spell *Parsifal*, which is where all nice opera queens spend Good Friday.

H) Though opera queens are on the ladylike side, there is no need to test them on this too strenuously. Without a chaperon, I, for one, wouldn't be caught dead with an opera queen in a parterre box at the Met.

I) Years spent in the company of characters famous for going mad at the drop of a handkerchief and ingenious in their suicide methods have given some opera queens rather, er, distinctive ideas about what sex is. Before you become, er, intimate with an opera queen, it is best to query him thoroughly about his tastes in sex lest you wind up being entombed or placed on a rock and surrounded by impenetrable fire. A little bondage is nifty, but draw the line at being placed in a burlap sack. Under no circumstances whatsoever go to a bullfight with an opera queen. Novices to opera should also be wary about an opera queen who asks, "Before we do it, would you like to try to answer a few riddles?" And run for the nearest exit when your request for a little kiss is met with "This is a kiss according to Tosca."

Cruising the Met is probably the most respectable way to meet fellow faggots. Being able to answer "At Jessye Norman's first Met *Ariadne auf Naxos*" instead of "At Sleaze Night at the baths" to the question "And where did you two meet?" not only sounds classy but helps keep up the myth of the homosexual as appreciator of life's "finer things." (There is never any need to mention that after *Ariadne auf Naxos*, you both tramped off to the baths to consummate your relationship.)

[*1989*]

Court
ship
& Commitment

THE DREYFUS AFFAIR

Peter Lefcourt

THE VIKINGS WON AGAIN SATURDAY NIGHT, 5–24. IN THE EIGHTH
D. J. Pickett punched a low outside forkball down the line between the first
baseman and the bag, bringing in two runs and putting the Vikings ahead
before the Huba Henry came out of the bullpen to nail it down. It was a
beautiful piece of hitting, a textbook example of going with the pitch.

The clubhouse was rowdy after the game. You'd think they'd won the
pennant the way the players were cracking jokes and snapping their
towels at one another's asses. It was like a fraternity-house party.

Randy sat quietly in front of his locker with a diet Coke. Glen Ephard
came over. "Charlie wants to see you in his office."

"Right."

"You miss a sign tonight or something?"

Randy shrugged. He didn't know why Charlie Gonse wanted to see
him. He wasn't in the mood for a Greek-salad chat right now. All he
wanted to do was get out of there and be with D. J. They were planning to
meet across the Bay in Chinatown for a late dinner. He got up, still in his
uniform bottoms and sweatshirt, and walked over to the manager's office.

Charlie Gonse looked up from his cottage cheese and fruit plate and
motioned for Randy to enter.

"Have a seat," he said, pushing the paper plate away disdainfully.
"This shit'll kill you faster than cholesterol. I swear the cottage cheese
tastes like it was scraped off an asbestos ceiling."

"You wanted to see me, Charlie?"

"No. I just called you in here to talk about cottage cheese." The manager was wearing a terry-cloth bathrobe, his head wrapped in a towel. He plugged a toothpick from a dispenser on his desk and started to go at his upper incisors.

"I'm going to lay it right on the line, Shovel. All right?"

"Yeah."

"You got your head up your ass."

"What?"

"You're not in the ball game. I don't know where the fuck you are but you're not between the foul lines."

"What're you talking about? We've won ten of the last twelve games. I've been hitting .432 over that period. I haven't made an error since Cleveland—"

"Numbers. That's all that shit is. Numbers. I'm talking about being in the game. I'm talking about standing out there and having a clue where the hell you are. I got to tell you Shovel, I look at you out there sometimes and I get the distinct impression you're on another planet."

Randy stared back at his manager, trying to control his anger. The fact that the guy was right had nothing to do with the fact that he didn't deserve this shit. What difference did it make to Charlie Gonse what planet Randy was on as long as he did his job?

"Tell me something. What was the count on D. J. before he hit the double down the line in the eight?"

Randy looked at him incredulously. What kind of dumb question was that? Who the fuck knew? D. J. probably didn't even know.

"See what I mean?"

"I don't keep track of counts."

"You lose track of the count, you lose track of the game. You remember the count on D. J., you remember what the guy threw him with that count, so next time you're up against him with bases loaded and you got the same count, you know what to expect. You understand what I'm saying?"

Randy nodded. There was no point in contradicting Charlie Gonse about this, or anything else, for that matter. The guy had to be right all the time. When he went to the bullpen in the ninth and the batter hit one out on his relief pitcher, he was still right. It was always someone else's fault.

"My nephew still didn't get that picture you were supposed to send him."

"I'll take care of it."

"Get your head out of your ass."

"Right."

"That's it. Over and out."

Later that night, at the restaurant in Chinatown, Randy asked D. J. what the count had been on him when he hit the double.

"Three-and-one."

"You remember that shit?"'

"I remember that one because I said to myself that Grigan always comes in three-and-one with a slider outside, and I'm going to go right."

A water chestnut slid off Randy's chopstick and fell on his aqua Lacoste shirt. He was all nerves. It was a miracle he could still play baseball. And play well, no less. He had gone 2-for-4 with a double that night. His average was up to .345.

Randy watched D. J. skillfully scoop up pork, mushrooms, and rice with his chopstick and manage to get it all in his mouth without spilling anything. He had terrific hands. When he scooped up a ground ball he did it in one continuous, graceful movement. Randy could watch him field ground balls all night long. He could watch him eat pork lo mein all night. There was no doubt about it: He was crazy about the guy.

He had never felt like this before, not even with Susie. With Susie, he had wanted to fuck her and then wake up at the ball game. It wasn't at all like that with D. J. He wanted to talk to him, to eat in Chinese restaurants, to go to the movies, to feed him perfectly on the double play, laying the ball in chest high so that he could pivot and avoid the spikes of the sliding runner. Most of all, he wanted to go back to the weight room.

It was already midnight, and they had a day game tomorrow. A crucial game with Oakland. They should be in bed, lights out. But he wasn't at all tired. He felt a wild exhilaration, an excitement he hadn't felt since he was eighteen.

They paid the bill, splitting it down the middle, and wandered around until they found a martial-arts double feature in a large, empty movie house. They sat alone all the way up in the rear balcony. Downstairs were a few other male couples.

After a while Randy and D. J. started to neck. It was wild. He hadn't made out in a movie theater since he felt up Janice Vaccario in the balcony of the Crest Theater in Glendale. They eventually stopped watching the movie altogether. When it got to heavy petting, they grabbed a cab back to the hotel.

They took separate elevators up to the tenth floor. Randy went to the ice machine and got a bucket of ice while D. J. closed the curtains and turned the rheostat down to dim the lights.

Randy let himself in with an extra key. D. J. put out the DO NOT DISTURB SIGN and deadbolted the door. Then he put a Sinatra cassette into his portable tape deck and disappeared into the bathroom. When he reappeared he had slipped into something he had bought at a North Beach leather shop during the team's last trip to the Bay Area.

"Jesus," Randy muttered, his breath taken away.

"You like it?"

"Yeah." Randy was nodding so furiously that it looked as if he had some sort of spasmodic tic. He stood there for a long moment admiring D. J. Pickett's outfit as the ice cubes melted in the bucket and the room began to spin gently in front of him.

The Man began to sing "Our Lady Is Here to Stay." The ice bucket slipped out of Randy's hand and fell to the floor with a wet, whooshing sound. The Rockies began to crumble. Gibraltar began to tumble. They were only made of clay. . . .

[1992]

NEW YORK IN JUNE

Brian Sloan

THE NEXT MORNING, ROGER AND I AWOKE SHORTLY AFTER NINE A.M.
in the same bed. Naked. We made our way, bleary-eyed, to the bathroom
and took a shower together. Naked. We ate some leftover pizza while
sitting on the floor Indian style. Naked. We probably would have stayed
naked for the rest of the day, the rest of the year if we had had the choice.
It was, however, day five of our stay, and time to return to the clothed
world of suburban Maryland.

Our trip back on the train was slightly more subdued this time, since
Mr. Carter was accompanying us. We sat together in a cluster of four seats
that faced one another at the end of the car. Mr. Carter sat across the aisle
from us, reading the current issue of the *New Yorker*. Looking out the
window at the blurry, industrial brown landscape of the Jersey meadow-
lands, I wondered about tomorrow—the tomorrow I had now, almost
unknowingly, gotten myself into on this field trip that was supposed to
have educated me about the art of journalism. I wondered how Roger
and I would hold up outside of the unreality of the past week. I wondered
if we would date and go to the movies. I wondered if it was somehow
possible to take him to the senior prom.

Halfway home, this pensive mood and existential questioning ceased
when a glamorous couple in their late twenties boarded the train in
Philadelphia and sat across from Mr. Carter. We learned that this couple
had just been married, and were starting their long journey to Miami
Beach for their honeymoon. The man was tall and dashingly handsome,

his looks verging on the ridiculousness of a Disney prince. The woman was equally attractive, but in a sassier way, her auburn hair wildly askew, resembling a funnier version of Cher.

On the seat next to Mr. Carter, they opened up a large wicker basket and started pulling out little white bags filled with exotic cheeses, baguettes, marinated vegetables, and cold cuts. They asked Mr. Carter if he would like to share their snacks. Peeking up from his magazine, he quietly demurred. Raul, however, was less polite; he said he would gladly take Mr. Carter's portion if he didn't want it. Roger piped in too, informing the couple that the four of us were with Mr. Carter. Cher cackled a bit, charmed by our audacity, and invited us to join their moveable feast.

We crossed to the other side of the train and crowded around their basket. As we munched on the gourmet snacks, we told the couple about our adventures in New York, censoring out the illegal parts in deference to Mr. Carter. Cher was duly impressed by our work at the paper, especially the abortion scandal, to which she uttered a hearty "Right on!" After seeing how much we could impress other adults, Mr. Carter lightened up a bit and started enjoying himself. He took a sort of parental pride in the four of us that would have been unthinkable five days before. He seemed to sense that something about us had changed. We had all aged, or, more appropriately, we had finally caught up with the ages that we already were.

With great flourish, The Prince opened a large bottle of wine and offered Mr. Carter some. To our shock, Mr. Carter accepted, and took a full Dixie cup. The Prince then offered me some. I looked over at Mr. Carter, expecting a look of disapproval, but instead he seemed pleased by the idea and said why the hell not? There was a great deal of laughter as The Prince passed three Dixie cups in our direction and filled them with a twist of his wrist. Barry declined at first, citing an uneasy stomach; but when Raul (who whispered, so as not to disturb the civility of this event) called him a lightweight pussy, Barry meekly asked Cher for another cup, his face breaking out in his trademark blush.

We all raised our Dixies in a circle, toasting their new marriage. Mr. Carter wished them a long, happy life together. The Prince said, "All righty!" with an exclamation point. Cher said, "Cheers," as she created a little tinkling noise with her bracelet to substitute for the dull sound of paper cups bumping into each other. After I took a sip, Roger turned to me, winked or blinked, smiled broadly, and made a toast to New York City. This time, I blushed.

It was official. There we were, adults sitting on a train drinking wine with other adults, who had actually *provided* the stuff. And the strange thing is that, unlike in our previous encounters with illegal liquor, none of us was barking, farting, yelling, or puking. We just sat there sipping, like regular human beings. Despite all the odds, some sort of maturity had seeped into us. For me, something else had seeped in: a growing aware-ness of love as an emotion and not some sort of juvenile joke. Simply put, Roger had seeped into my life, and into my heart as well. But I don't have the time or space to get into that. It's a whole different story.

It's the story of my life.

[1994]

FEARLESS

Jameson Currier

THEY MET AGAIN ON SATURDAY TO SEE A MOVIE IN THE VILLAGE. David was already at the corner of Bleecker Street when Barry arrived and greeted him with a kiss on the lips. David gave Barry a weak and embarrassed smile, and as they walked together toward the theater, Barry took hold of David's hand. David, surprised, looked down at their hands, joined at his side, as if it were a scar or a blemish he were not supposed to acknowledge but *had* to inspect. David had never been comfortable with such open public affection between men, and he wondered now if Barry had misread him from their rainy walk from last week. He looked out at the people passing them on the sidewalk, hoping to spot another male couple holding hands, but all he saw were startled expressions, eyes focused in their direction, right at their hands. David moved their joined arms so that their hands fell behind his back as they walked, trying to rationalize his timidity and uneasiness. Wasn't Barry's public affection just another thing he had to overcome or adjust to, like his youth and smoking and sero-status? Weren't they, after all, walking in the *Village?* Wasn't this *their* part of town? Finally, however, worried by the stares they were still receiving, David just let go of Barry's hand, knowing it must *really* look queer to be *holding* hands and *hiding* them.

By now David had reached a foolish state of confusion. He had not dated anyone in over nine months, not since his blitz period—the period he had answered personal ads, joined a dating club, and started calling a phone line—the results of which were too many dates with too many wrong guys. But even in his younger days, even when he had been Barry's age, David had never been able to master the protocols of dating. He had never known when to be aggressive, when to wait for a phone call, when to flirt with someone or how to catch a stare on the street. In those days he had felt awkward and unattractive, always standing on the outside of gay life; even the clues and codes mystified him—what were all those keys and colored handkerchiefs *really* about anyway? But sex had always been obtainable for him—he was always approached at the bars or the baths; in fact, he went to those places to find reassurances that he was *not* awkward and unattractive. In those days dating to him meant having sex. Sex, sex, sex. It's why he got together with a guy for a second time. No matter what incompatibilities there were, sex was an action that made them compatible, even if only briefly.

Now, everything about Barry bewildered David—the touching, the holding hands in public, the fuzzy feelings David felt inside while they were together. But David also thought that with Barry he had not made any progress after all these years; what did they have in common with each other, really, besides their desire to have sex with one another? David had hoped that by now, at his age and having survived this far into the plague, he would have reached something *beyond* a sexual relationship. Was he merely using Barry as reassurance of his own attractiveness or was he instead simply smitten by the attentiveness? Was he afraid of falling in love or worse, falling in love and being abandoned, or even more worse, falling in love and watching someone die? Was the real issue Barry's sero-status? Or had David accepted that through the act of sex? Or was David simply *incapable* of a relationship? But David could even justify now that Barry wasn't physically even his *type*. Wasn't David, after all, attracted and more interested in guys his own height and age—those boyish, actorish friends, conservative and nonthreatening, who knew the same subjects he did, could talk in the same shorthand about the theater or books or movies? But even this was discouraging; somehow everyone David knew or met these days was already attached to someone richer or better looking or taller or smarter.

Perhaps what David needed *was* someone younger, someone uninhibited and dauntless.

Though Barry was first drawn to David because of his boyish looks, Barry knew he and David were really not compatible. And it had nothing to do with David's age, nothing to do with David's reticence or over-educated response to everything. Emotionally Barry found himself drawn to men who were adventurous and willing to take risks, the reason why he was captivated by the spontaneity of the club crowd, those ready to just go out there and dance and sweat it out. But physically he was wildly attracted, too, to those macho-masculine men who were tall and unapproachable-looking, rough around the edges, the straight construction worker-cowboy types, the kind who presented as much danger as discipline. "In other words, someone unavailable," a woman in his support group had laughed the night Barry had explained this. That was the first group Barry had left. He had changed therapists for the same reason when, in a session, his doctor suggested that perhaps what he was searching for was a surrogate for the father he felt had abandoned him.

When Barry had brought the subject of David up at his support group meeting that week, Ken, an older man who believed he specialized in being dumped—even older than David—warned Barry to be prepared for the worst. "People don't change," Ken said. "If he hesitates now, he'll hesitate later." Justin, a year younger than Barry, yelled at Barry and said he should just forget about David. "It's his fault, anyway, man," Justin said. "They fucked around for years. Those kind of guys gave us AIDS." That prompted an argument within the group, angry cross-examinations and challenges displacing Barry's desire for advice.

Earlier that week, when David had phoned his friend Stuart and asked if he, Stuart, would ever date someone who was positive, there followed that notorious gap of silence. By the time Stuart spoke, David already knew his answer.

"You're putting your life at risk," Stuart said. "No one else. *You* have to make that choice."

When David pressed him harder, what would Stuart *do*, Stuart again avoided the question. "I have a lover," Stuart said. "I'm lucky I don't have to be out there."

David called his friend Wes in Los Angeles and asked him the same question. This time there was no hesitation. "No," Wes said bluntly. David and Wes had slept together years ago. Now Wes worked for an organization that raised funds for AIDS research. When David pressed Wes to explain his decision, Wes answered succinctly, "I can't work with it *and* live with it." Later, toward the end of their conversation, Wes asked David, "Do you feel something for him?"

"Yes," David answered honestly, but then he remembered he had also felt something for John-Boy on "The Waltons" and Michael on "thirtysomething."

David wished Barry was negative. Barry wished David was positive.

They held hands throughout the movie.

Afterwards, Barry took David home to his apartment on the Upper East Side.

[1994]

GOOD BOYS
Paul Reidinger

DAWN PALES THE EASTERN SKY WHEN CARL FINDS HIM, CRUMPLED on the couch like a thrown-away doll. All his clothes are on except his shoes, which are lined up neatly by the door.

The energy kick of the MDA is beginning to wear off now, but Carl's senses are fully alive: He is aware of himself. Chris: A beautiful thing, even tangled up as he is. Carl feels a tremendous surge of hot affection for the boy. So this is where he went! At first Carl thought he had just gone for a glass of juice; by the time he failed to return, Carl was already buzzing from hits of this and that (plus the MDA, which he'd taken in the bathroom, up the ass, shortly before they'd left the apartment; Chris did not know this). From time to time, it flashed across his eyes that he hadn't seen Chris in a while, but like a firefly's light, recognition of the absence quickly faded, and he went back to his dancing and his friends, speeding the night away.

"Sweet prince," he murmurs, bending to kiss Chris on the lips. Hunger and the urge for caffeine command him, however, and in a moment he is in the kitchen, grinding Guatemalan coffee beans in the Braun grinder and rummaging through the refrigerator for omelet ingredients. As the sun finally peeks above the Berkeley hills, its first light glinting red off the miniblinds but soon growing warm and white, he loads his big breakfast onto a tray and takes it into the bedroom so he can watch a porno movie while he eats.

Ever since the terrible crackle-screech of the coffee grinder Chris has been awake, groggy at first and uncertain of where exactly he is, then remembering, feeling utterly degraded, trapped in the apartment of a man he no longer wants to have anything to do with. He pretended to be asleep while he was trying to figure out how to escape; now Carl is in the bedroom, and if there is to be a window of opportunity, this must be it.

Shoes are by the door—right where he left them. He can pick them up and rush out into the morning without putting them on, without having to deal with Carl; he can put them on in the car. The plan is terribly simple, foolproof, impossible to bungle. He sits up and eyes the shoes.

Last night he told himself he was too tired to drive the forty-five minutes to his own place, even though it wasn't even three o'clock and he wasn't the least bit drunk and had often made the drive even deeper in the night, when all the circumstances were far worse. It made sense, he told himself last night, that he should sleep at Carl's—carefully establishing himself on the sofa to emphasize *at Carl's*, not *with Carl*.

It makes sense, therefore, to leave without saying anything. There is nothing to say. The evening was a predictable catastrophe. Only the final indignity of Carl's coming home with some other man in tow has been avoided; he seems to be in there alone.

Yawning, Chris gets to his feet and pads into the toilet, where he pees quite audibly. *I don't care*, he says to himself. *Let him listen*. Having made up his mind not to play dead anymore, he is filled with reckless defiance. The whole thing has been a grievous mistake—three months wasted.

"Three months wasted," he hears himself saying. He looks up from the porcelain bowl and sees Carl's face reflected in the mirror over the washbasin. It is a haggard and white face, dark rings under red eyes: drugs warmed over. Carl's expression is infinitely sad, but peaceful, like a martyr's. Calmly, Chris buttons himself up and flushes, wondering how he is going to deal with this new obstacle. It's one thing just to disappear— here one minute, gone the next; quite another to barge wordlessly past someone you've been sleeping with for weeks, as if he didn't exist.

In that moment of hesitation, Carl speaks. "I'm sorry," he says.

Chris glances at him in the mirror, conscious of a sudden weakening in his knees. Carl looks vulnerable, tired, in need of a hug.

"Me too," Chris says, turning.

"I didn't know what happened to you."

"You didn't even look."

"No," Carl says, mortified. "I kept thinking you'd come back. We were all pretty fucked up. I wasn't sure you weren't right behind me somewhere."

"I wasn't."

"I know that. I'm sorry."

"I just can't stand this," Chris said. "You did it deliberately, so you wouldn't really have to be with me. You let your friends take over so you don't have to deal with change in your life. You're afraid of your own feelings."

Carl's head droops, but he holds out his arms toward Chris. "I really am sorry," he says in a pathetic whisper.

For an awkward moment they stand like that: Carl with his arms extended, Chris frozen next to the toilet. Gradually Carl's arms sag, as though the muscles, like those in his neck, are leaking air.

"I love you," Chris says in a flat, hard voice—a challenge. Carl does not look up. "I wish I didn't. I mean, it's hopeless. But I do. I don't know what to do." He steps through the narrow space between Carl and the doorjamb, expecting Carl to touch him, which he does not. He sits on the low bench by the front door and works the laces of his sneakers.

"I know it's mostly my fault," Carl says. He has followed at a contrite distance and is now sitting on the opposite end of the bench. "This isn't easy for me, you know. I like my bad habits! I've had them a long time. I'm perfect at them. What am I supposed to say to all these people I know? Sorry, can't see you anymore? They're like family."

"You don't even try."

"Nothing I could try would satisfy you anyway," Carl says. "Face it. You have this rigid idea of what we have to be. You can't see it any other way."

"I love you," Chris says, "and you don't love me."

"You know it's not that simple."

"It is." The shoes are laced and tied; he is ready to go, but he doesn't. "You're wrong."

Chris stands.

"Please don't go," Carl murmurs. "Please don't leave me."

You're too fucked up on drugs to know what you're saying, Chris thinks—but something stops him from saying it. Carl is shuddering softly, making strange sniffly noises, and after a perplexed instant Chris understands that he's crying. He watches the bare shoulders quiver and heave, the muscles in the nape of the neck tense. Slowly he sinks back to the bench, one arm sliding involuntarily around Carl, the big warm mass settling under his shoulder. It is only decent to settle him down a little before leaving, Chris thinks, trying to ignore the sensual duet the two of them cannot seem to help playing, even when all hope is lost. Only decent.

[1993]

GIANT PACIFIC OCTOPUS

Edward Field

I live with a giant pacific octopus:
he settles himself down beside me on the couch in the evening.
With two arms he holds a book
that he reads with his single eye:
he wears a pair of glasses over it for reading.

Two more arms go walking over to the sideboard across the room
where the crackers and cheese spread he loves are,
and they send back endless canapés, like a conveyor belt.

While his mouth is drooling and chomping,
another arm comes over and gropes me lightly:
it is like a breeze on my balls, that sweet tentacle.

Other arms start slipping around my body under my clothes.
They wiggle right in, one around my waist,
and all over, and down the crack of my ass.

I am drawn into his midst where his hot mouth waits for kisses
and I kiss him and make him into a boy
as all giant pacific octopuses are really
when you take them into your arms.

All their arms fluttering around you
become everywhere sensations of pleasure.
So, his sweet eye looks at me and his little mouth kisses me
and I swear he had the body of a greek god,
my giant pacific octopus boychik.

So this was what was in store
when I first saw him in the aquarium
huddled miserably on the rock
ignoring the feast of live crabs
they put in his windowed swimming pool.

You take home a creature like that, who needs love,
who is a mess when you meet
but who can open up like a flower with petal arms waving
    around—a beauty—
and it is a total pleasure to have him around,
even collapsible as he is like a big toy,
for as long as he will stay, one night or a lifetime,
for as long as god will let you have him.

[1992]

THE MYSTERIES OF PITTSBURGH

Michael Chabon

WE SLEPT TOGETHER. HE WOULD GET UP IN THE MORNING AND RUSH off to work, scrabbling through piles of our mingled trousers and briefs, running his head under the sink, slamming the front door in farewell, and after he was gone I would spend the luxury of my extra hour by bathing in the Weatherwoman's claw-foot tub and in the strangeness of it all. We lived well. Arthur cooked elaborate dinners; in the refrigerator there was always pasta in the colors of the Italian flag, a variety of weird wines, capers, kiwis, unheard-of-fish with Hawaiian names, and stacks of asparagus, Arthur's favorite food, in the rubber-banded bundles that he never failed to refer to as fagots. We sent our dirty clothes out to be cleaned and they came back as gifts, tied up in blue paper. And, as often as possible, we went to bed. I did not consider myself to be gay; I did not consider myself, as a rule. But all day long, from the white instant when I opened my eyes in the morning until my last black second of awareness of Arthur's fading breath on my shoulder, I was always nervous, full of energy, afraid. The city was new again, and newly dangerous, and I would walk its streets quickly, eyes averted from those of passersby, like a spy in the employ of lust and happiness, carrying the secret deep within me but always on the tip of my tongue.

The rich young couple—who were due to return on the last day of July—employed a black woman to clean their house. Her name was Velva. At eight o'clock on my only Wednesday morning at the Weatherwoman House, she entered the bedroom and screamed. After a moment of keen observation, she ran from the room, shouting that she was sorry. Arthur and I separated, went soft, laughed. We lit cigarettes and discussed strategy.

"Maybe I should go downstairs," he said.

"Put some pants on."

"What will she do?" he said. "I don't know her well enough to predict. Black people confuse me."

"Pick up the extension."

"Why?"

"Maybe she's calling the police."

"Or an ambulance."

I thought of my fat friends from Boardwalk, arriving in their van to attach their electric paddles to the outraged, apoplectic cleaning lady collapsed on the living-room floor. Arthur picked up the extension, listened, set it down again.

"Dial tone," he said. "And I'm not going downstairs. You go. Slip her a five or something." He pushed me, and I fell out of bed, trailing the bedclothes behind me. A tendril of cotton blanket wrapped itself around a lamp, pulled the lamp to the floor after it, and then muffled the *bang!* of the shattered light bulb. We stared at each other, eyes round, muscles tensed, listening, like two boys who have been warned not to wake the baby. But the pop of the bulb was the incident's only repercussion. Velva contrived to be in another part of the house throughout our respective breakfasts and departures, and subsequent events indicated that she never said anything to anyone. Perhaps she did not care—I fantasized that she was Lurch's long-resigned mother. In any case, we were lucky. Like any successful spy, I felt frightened and lucky all the time.

Pittsburgh, too, was in the grip of a humid frenzy. The day after my flip of the coin, the sun had disappeared behind a perpetual gray wall of vapor, which never managed to form itself into rain, and yet the sun's heat remained as strong as ever, so that the thick, wet, sulfury air seemed to boil around you, and in the late morning veils of steam rose from the blacktop. Arthur said it was like living on Venus. When I walked to work—arriving sapped and with my damp shirt an alien thing clinging to me—the Cathedral of Learning, ordinarily brown, would look black with wetness, dank, submerged, Atlantean. There were three irrational shootings that week, and two multiple-car pileups on the freeway; a Pirate, in a much-discussed lapse of sportsmanship, broke three teeth belonging to a hapless Phillie; a live infant was found in a Bloomfield garbage can.

And in bed, as our last week in the Weatherwoman House drew to a close, our dealings with each other became distinctly more Venusian. The stranglehold, the bite, and even the light blow, found their way into our sexual repertoire: I discovered purple marks along the tops of my shoulders. It's the weather, I said to myself; or else, I added—once, and for only an instant, since I was so firmly opposed to consideration—this is just the way it is with another man.

[1988]

WHEN YOU GROW TO ADULTERY

David Leavitt

ANDREW WAS IN LOVE WITH JACK SELDEN, SO ALL JACK'S LITTLE habits, his particular ways of doing things, seemed marvelous to him: the way Jack put his face under the shower, after shampooing his hair, and shook his head like a big dog escaped from a bath; the way he slept on his back, his arms crossed in the shape of a butterfly over his face, fists on his eyes; his fondness for muffins and Danish and sweet rolls—what he called, at first just out of habit and then *because* it made Andrew laugh, "baked goods." Jack made love with efficient fervor, his face serious, almost businesslike. Not that he was without affection, but everything about him had an edge; his very touch had an edge, there was the possibility of pain lurking behind every caress. It seemed to Andrew that Jack's touches, more than any he'd known before, were full of meaning—they sought to express, not just to please or explore—and this gesturing made him want to gesture back, to enter into a kind of tactile dialogue. They'd known each other only a month, but already it felt to Andrew as if their fingers had told each other novels.

Andrew had gone through most of his life not being touched by anyone, never being touched at all. These days, his body under the almost constant scrutiny of two distinct pairs of hands, seemed to him perverse punishment, as if he had had a wish granted and was now suffering the consequences of having stated the wish too vaguely. He actually envisioned, sometimes, the fairy godmother shrugging her shoulder and saying, "You get what you ask for." Whereas most of his life he had been alone, unloved, now he had two lovers—Jack for just over a month, and Allen for close to three years. There was no cause and effect, he insisted, but had to admit things with Allen had been getting ragged around the edges for some time. Jack and Allen knew about each other and had agreed to endure, for the sake of the undecided Andrew, a tenuous and open-ended period of transition, during which Andrew himself spent so much of his time on the subway, riding between the two apartments of his two lovers, that it began to seem to him as if rapid transit was the true and final home of the desired. Sometimes he wanted nothing more than to crawl into the narrow bed of his childhood and revel in the glorious, sad solitude of no one—not even his mother—needing or loving him. Hadn't the hope of future great loves been enough to curl up against? It seemed so now. His skin felt soft, toneless, like the skin of a plum poked by too many housewifely hands, feeling for the proper ripeness; he was covered with fingerprints.

This morning he had woken up with Jack—a relief. One of the many small tensions of the situation was that each morning, when he woke up, there was a split second of panic as he sought to reorient himself and figure out where he was, who he was with. It was better with Jack, because Jack was new love and demanded little of him; with Allen, lately, there'd been thrashing, by heavy breathing, by a voice whispering in his ear, "Tell me one thing. Did you promise Jack we wouldn't have sex? I have to know."

"No, I didn't."

"Thank God, thank God. Maybe now I can go back to sleep."

There was a smell of coffee. Already showered and dressed for work (he was an architect at a spiffy firm), Jack walked over to the bed, smiling, and kissed Andrew, who felt rumpled and sour and unhappy. Jack's mouth carried the sweet taste of coffee, his face was smooth and newly shaven and still slightly wet. "Good morning," he said.

"Good morning."

"I love you," Jack Selden said.

Immediately Allen appeared, crushed, devastated, in a posture of crucifixion against the bedroom wall. "My God," he said, "you're killing me, you know that? You're killing me."

It was Rosh Hashanah, and Allen had taken the train out the night before to his parents' house in New Jersey. Andrew was supposed to join him that afternoon. He looked up now at Jack, smiled, then closed his eyes. His brow broke into wrinkles. "Oh God," he said to Jack, putting his arms around his neck, pulling him closer, so that Jack almost spilled his coffee, "now I have to face Allen's family."

Jack kissed Andrew on the forehead before pulling gingerly from his embrace. "I still can't believe Allen told them," he said, sipping more coffee from a mug which said WORLD'S GREATEST ARCHITECT. Jack had a mostly perfunctory relationship with his own family—hence the mug, a gift from his mother.

"Yes," Andrew said. "But Sophie's hard to keep secrets from. She sees him, and she knows something's wrong, and she doesn't give in until he's told her."

"Listen, I'm sure if he told you she's not going to say anything, she's not going to say anything. Anyway, it'll be fun, Andrew. You've told me a million times how much you enjoy big family gatherings."

"Easy for you to say. You get to go to your nice clean office and work all day and sleep late tomorrow and go out for brunch." Suddenly Andrew sat up in bed. "I don't think I can take this anymore, this running back and forth between you and him." He looked up at Jack shyly. "Can't I stay with you? In your pocket?"

Jack smiled. Whenever he and his last boyfriend, Ralph, had had something difficult to face—the licensing exam, or a doctor's appointment—they would say to each other, "Don't worry, I'll be there with you. I'll be in your pocket." Jack had told Andrew, who had in turn appropriated the metaphor, but Jack didn't seem to mind. He smiled down at Andrew—he was sitting on the edge of the bed now, smelling very clean, like hair tonic—and brushed his hand over Andrew's forehead. Then he reached down to the breast pocket of his own shirt, undid the little button there, pulled it open, made a plucking gesture over Andrew's face, as if he were pulling off a loose eyelash, and bringing his hand back, rubbed his fingers together over the open pocket, dropping something in.

"You're there," he said. "You're in my pocket."

"All day?" Andrew asked.

"All day." Jack smiled again. And Andrew, looking up at him, said, "I love you," astonished even as he said the words at how dangerously he was teetering on the brink of villainy.

[1990]

SUCH TIMES

Christopher Coe

THE NIGHT JASPER TOLD ME HE HAD NOT EVER HEARD ANYONE GO ON in quite the way that I did on our first date, at the Greek place, was an August night. It was years later, 1980 or '81, I think. We were in Province-town, our third or fourth time there. It was late, after dinner and after an after-dinner drink. We were talking out on a long jetty built of boulders, huge uneven stones, a massive effort made by hardy, enterprising people many years before. It extends out over the bay.

Jasper and I had walked out on this stone jetty half a dozen times, always at night, without ever getting to the point where it stops. In daylight, on bicycles, we could see how long it was—it goes a long way out over the water. At night, walking on it, we had no idea how far we had come.

It took an effort to get out even as far as we did, more than just walk-ing; you had to jump the rocks, or climb up between them, and you had to watch your footing.

Jasper, who was far more agile than I will ever be, was faster over the rocks. He'd always get ahead of me, and he'd stop, every fifty feet or so, and wait for me to catch up to him. Then he'd be off again. In one or two places, Jasper had to pull me up between the rocks. This pier was not a promenade for me.

Sometimes, when Jasper was far ahead of me, I wished I could be more agile for him. I wished I had for him an athlete's grace, that I could just glide over the rocks, swiftly, with ease, as though they were a path to lead me to him. I wished that I could be, for him, his able, agile, good-looking young boy.

That night, we got out far enough to leave the world behind, away from the bars, the discos, the boisterousness of too many people having all the fun they could manage. We got ourselves away from all that.

Farther than we'd been before, we found a rock smooth enough to lie on, so we lay down on it. We looked up, into the night, through a canopy of stars. They seemed themselves bewildered at being where they were, to have been burning so long, alive all their millions of years.

We were quite awhile with each other in the immensity. We lay close together, and Jasper produced from a pocket a thin silver flask. It had a small cap to use as a cup. We sipped green Chartreuse from this and tasted it on each other's lips, from each other's mouths.

"Yours is better than mine," Jasper said.

"You think?" I asked, and tasted his.

"I know," Jasper said.

"I like yours more," I said. "Give me some of yours."

"This is a nice way to drink Chartreuse," Jasper said.

"Give me more of yours," I said.

The sky, which had been clear, became even clearer. Jasper told me he had never seen such a multitude of stars. Nor had I, I told him, and it was true: I hadn't. Jasper began to name a few of them, some constellations that he knew—the Big Dipper, the Pleiades, Aldebaron.

"Hush," I said. "Give me more of yours."

He did.

We had many fine evenings. There were winter evenings in New York with Montecruz 210s and Irish coffee with real cream. There were summer sunsets with champagne framboise on the Quai d'Orléans. Now the fine evenings seem fewer—though I know that they were many. They may also now seem finer than they were. If I exaggerate, I do so only a little. There were nights with Jasper, many nights, and days, that gave me almost all that I had ever dared to want. The evening with the stars and with the green Chartreuse is only one of them.

[1993]

"À LA RECHERCHE DE GERTRUDE STEIN"

Frank O'Hara

When I am feeling depressed and anxious sullen
all you have to do is take your clothes off
and all is wiped away revealing life's tenderness
that we are flesh and breathe and are near us
as you are really as you are I become as I
really am alive and knowing vaguely what is
and what is important to me above the intrusions
of incident and accidental relationships
which have nothing to do with my life

when I am in your presence I feel life is strong
and will defeat all its enemies and all of mine
and all of yours and yours in you and mine in me
sick logic and feeble reasoning are cured
by the perfect symmetry of your arms and legs
spread out making an eternal circle together
creating a golden pillar beside the Atlantic
the faint line of hair dividing your torso
gives my mind rest and emotions their release
into the infinite air where since once we are
together we always will be in this life come what may

[1959]

SURPRISING MYSELF

Christopher Bram

WHAT WERE WE?

I took a deep breath, hoping to get the smell of Corey's hair and soap and sweat, but my nose was too accustomed to us now to smell anything.

We were friends, partners. We were lovers, only neither of us liked the word: me because it sounded mushy and temporary, Corey because it had exploitative connotations. We lived together. We had come a long way together, too long for me to lie here wondering who we were. We were Joel and Corey, simple as that. For me to wonder about that was as goofy as picking up a spoon and wondering why it was a spoon, why it was this spoon and not another spoon, turning its very existence into a puzzle, a mystery. And yet, it was something like that which had spoiled the sex for me, as if I'd grabbed too hard at a spoon I was afraid might not be there.

Corey lay there with his eyes closed, lightly drawing circles on my back.

"Core? Do I always seem real to you?"

His eyes stayed contentedly closed. "Real? Very real."

"Seriously. Do you feel like I'm really here? Metaphysically."

It was the wrong word: Corey grinned. "You mean like, are you an illusion? Am I dreaming you? Is reality only a movie projected by God? Berkeley and all that?"

"Something like that. But not—"

"Well, I refuse you thus," and he blindly kissed me on the cheek.

There are things you can't discuss with someone who minored in philosophy; they turn it into something they've studied. "But more real than that. More physical and strange."

The anxiety showed in my voice; he suddenly opened his eyes.

"I don't know how to describe it better, only. . . Do you know what I'm talking about?"

"Maybe. I'm not sure." He sounded worried. "I don't take you for granted. Is that what you mean? I care very much about you. You know that."

"I know. And I care about you. But it's not that." In his usual Cobbetty fashion, he was afraid he had done something wrong. "It's more. . ." I patted my hands around an empty space the size of a basketball. "More like—" What was it like? "When you stare at a word too long and it begins to look misspelled? Yes, like that. A word you use everyday and you find yourself looking at it so hard that it's nothing but letters. Until you have to look it up in the dictionary before you can be sure it's really a word."

"Hmmm." He sounded amused by it, not threatened. "And I'm looking misspelled to you?"

"Just tonight. And not just you. But things. Us." I was afraid I'd said something very terrible. "Haven't I ever looked misspelled to you, Boy?"

He seriously thought about it and I began to feel foolish.

"Now and then," he finally admitted. "But especially in the beginning." He sheepishly lowered his voice. "When I was *in* love with you. Before I loved you."

Corey was ashamed of the distinction he made between love and in love. It was like confessing he wasn't in love with me anymore, that he only loved me. That didn't hurt me because I didn't believe in his categories; I couldn't separate the two emotions in myself. I felt Corey separated them only to explain to himself the differences between his initial, difficult love for me, and the love that finally succeeded. I liked to think of his notion of two loves as an emblem of what we'd come through together.

"I love you," I said. "But I'm still in love with you, too."

"Yes. I know." He paused over his refusal to say the same. He was too scrupulously sincere to say it. "But I remember being with you and being overwhelmed with whys and whats and who-is-this-guy, especially when you were sleeping. It wasn't the bad doubting I used later. It was more like wonder and sort of exciting. I thought I was so rational and yet there I was, up to my nose in the ineffable."

"It is exciting," I admitted. "In an unnerving kind of way. But you can still feel it? Now and then, you said."

"Oh yeah. Like right now. Just talking about it makes me feel, oh, epistomologically spacey." He happily gathered me against his side, as if I were all that was needed to fill that space. "I'm sure you've felt it before too."

"Not like this." And not after sex. Sex usually answered any questions. But I was feeling better, now that we were talking and Corey didn't think I was crazy. Telling him I loved and was in love made my confusion easier to bear. I began to feel silly, as if I'd been fretting about something that everyone else knew how to handle.

"Maybe it's just your situation," said Corey. "We're over here, we just moved and aren't settled yet. You don't know what you'll be doing. Everything's so up in the air for you right now."

I smiled. "But I have you," I said. "You're all the situation I need."

Corey laughed. "No wonder you're confused. I'm misspelled to begin with. But my situation is better than yours. Because I have you."

"A ditz who has to ask if he's real?" I laughed at myself. "Uh uh. I'm the lucky one. I'm the one who got better than he deserves."

We teased each other and that settled everything. Insisting we didn't deserve each other proved that we knew otherwise. We could be silly together, confessing our faults—my sudden quirks, Corey's self-consciousness, my stub of a nose, Corey's big feet—until I felt good enough to let him go so he could shut himself in the bathroom. Corey needed a few minutes alone after doing what we did.

I thought about taking the butter dish back to the kitchen: It'd be difficult explaining its presence here tomorrow. But I sat there on the empty sofa with my arms around my knees, thinking about love. Because, without his body there to distract me, it was obvious what I'd been feeling.

I'd said it myself: I was still in love with Corey. The fear or doubt or desperate whatever that had spoiled the sex didn't seem so bad to me now. I was still in love and my furious expectations had only been my response to something that had never explained itself away, never lost its power to amaze me. After all this time. I should be pleased with that. Shouldn't I?

Almost three years, and I could still surprise myself with my love for Corey, love for a guy, love in general. I had spent so much of my life being surprised by others. I preferred the surprises I gave to myself.

[1987]

AUTHOR BIOGRAPHIES

CHRISTOPHER BRAM, originally from Virginia, has lived in New York City since 1978. His novels include *Hold Tight, In Memory of Angel Clare*, and his most recent, *Father of Frankenstein*, based on the life of James Whale, the director of the original film *Frankenstein*. He also writes screenplays, book and film reviews, and contributed to *Hometowns*.

LIAM BROSNAHAN's fiction has appeared in several magazines including *McCall's* and *Christopher Street* and in the literary anthologies *Men on Men 5* and *Not the Only One*. He lives in New York.

PETER CAMERON is the best-selling author of the novels *Leap Year* and *The Weekend*, as well as two collections of short stories, *One Way or Another* and *Far-flung*. He works for the Lambda Legal Defense Fund in New York City and is currently at work on a new novel.

MICHAEL CHABON made an astonishing literary debut at the age of twenty-four with *The Mysteries of Pittsburg*. He went on to write *A Model World & Other Stories* and the novel *Wonder Boys*. His stories have appeared in the *New Yorker* and *Mademoiselle*, among other publications.

CHRISTOPHER COE's novels, *I Look Divine* and *Such Times*, were both published to wide acclaim. He died of AIDS-related complications in 1994 at the age of forty-one.

MICHAEL CUNNINGHAM is the author of the highly praised novel *A Home at the End of the World*. His most recent novel is *Flesh & Blood*. A native of Southern California, he currently lives in New York City.

JAMESON CURRIER is the author of *Dancing on the Moon: Short Stories about AIDS* and writer of the documentary film *Living Proof: HIV and the Pursuit of Happiness*. His writings about AIDS and the gay community have appeared in a variety of publications, including the *Washington Post, Los Angeles Times, Art & Understanding*, and the anthologies *Certain Voices, All the Ways Home*, and *Men on Men 5*.

DANIEL CURZON has been a pioneer in the modern gay literary movement since his first book, *Something You Do in the Dark*, was published in 1971. His other books include *The Revolt of Perverts, Human Warmth & Other Stories*, and, most recently, *Superfag*. He lives in San Francisco.

DAVID B. FEINBERG's books include *Eighty-Sixed* and *Queer & Loathing: Rants & Raves of a Raging AIDS Clone*.

EDWARD FIELD's first book of poetry, *Stand Up, Friend, With You*, won the Lamont Award in 1962. His other books include *A Full Heart* and *Counting Myself Lucky: Selected Poems, 1963–1992*. He also wrote the narration for the 1965 Academy Award–winning documentary *To Be Alive*. He lives in New York.

STEPHEN FRY is best known to American audiences for his roles in Masterpiece Theater's series *Jeeves and Wooster* and the film *Peter's Friends*. In addition to his acting credits he has written a play entitled *Latin*, the book for the musical *Me and My Girl*, and a weekly column in the *London Daily Telegraph*. His most recent novel is *The Hippopotamus*. He lives in London and Norfolk.

MICHAEL GRUMLEY, together with his partner Robert Ferro, founded the writers' group The Violet Quill. He is also the author of *There Are Giants in the Earth, Hard Corps*, and *After Midnight*. He died of AIDS in 1988.

E. LYNN HARRIS was a computer sales executive for IBM before publishing his first novel, *Invisible Life*, in 1991. His other novels are *Just As I Am* and the best-selling *And This Too Shall Pass*.

JOHN EDWARD HARRIS was born and raised in Iowa. He lives in New York where he works as an editor at *Theatre Week* and is currently at work on a novel.

PATRICK HOCTEL is a writer and editor who lives and works in San Francisco. He has written for the *San Francisco Sentinel, SF Weekly, European Gay Review* and *Bay Area Reporter*, where he is currently an assistant editor. His work has appeared in *Christopher Street, The James White Review, Mirage, Tribe, modern words* and the anthologies *Men on Men 1, Certain Voices*, and *In the Company of My Solitude: American Writing From the AIDS Pandemic*.

ANDREW HOLLERAN is the author of two novels, *Dancer from the Dance* and *Nights in Aruba,* and a book of essays, *Ground Zero.* He currently writes a monthly column for *Christopher Street.*

ALAN HOLLINGHURST is the author of the highly praised novel *The Swimming Pool Library.* In 1993 he was selected by *Granta* as one of the Best Young British Novelists. He is on the staff of the *Times Literary Supplement.*

FENTON JOHNSON, a recipient of numerous awards for his fiction and nonfiction, is the author of two novels, *Crossing the River* and *Scissors, Paper, Rock.* He is a frequent contributor to the *New York Times Magazine* and teaches creative writing at San Francisco State University. His most recent book is *Geography of the Heart: A Memoir.*

FRANCIS KING has written over twenty novels, including *Voices in an Empty Room, The Man on the Rock,* and *Punishments.* His nonfiction work includes *E. M. Forster and His World* and *Florence.*

DAVID LEAVITT is the best-selling author of *Family Dancing, The Lost Language of Cranes,* and *While England Sleeps,* among other novels and collections of stories. His latest book, *Italian Pleasures,* was written in collaboration with Mark Mitchell. He is currently living in Rome.

PETER LEFCOURT is an Emmy Award–winning writer and producer for movies and television. He is also the author of *The Deal* and, most recently, *Di & I: A Novel.* He lives in Los Angeles and Paris.

STAN LEVENTHAL was an author, editor, publisher, and activist. His stories and reviews appeared in various journals including *Outweek* and *The Advocate.* He edited *Torso Magazine* and is the author of several books, including *Mountain Climbing in Sheridan Square, Skydiving on Christopher Street,* and *A Herd of Tiny Elephants.* He died of AIDS on January 15, 1995. His last book, *Barbie in Bondage,* was published posthumously in April 1996.

ARMISTEAD MAUPIN'S *Tales of the City* began as a serial novel first appearing in the *San Francisco Chronicle* in 1976. The serial produced six novels in total that have sold more than two million copies worldwide. He has been living in San Francisco since 1971 and is currently at work on a new novel entitled *The Crooked Thing.*

STEPHEN MCCAULEY lives in Cambridge, Massachusetts. His three novels, *The Object of My Affection, The Easy Way Out,* and *The Man of The House,* have all been published to critical and popular acclaim.

TERRENCE MCNALLY has written several plays and television scripts including *A Perfect Ganesh, Frankie and Johnnie in the Claire de Lune,* the book for the musical *Kiss of the Spider Woman,* and, most recently, *Master Class.* He has been the recipient of two Guggenheim Fellowships, a Rockefeller Grant, and a citation from the American Academy of Arts and Letters.

JAMES MERRILL won almost every major prize awarded for poetry, including the Pulitzer, the National Book Award, and the Bollingen for his collections *Nights and Days, Braving the Elements, Divine Comedies,* and *The Changing Light at Sandover.* His coming-of-age memoir, *A Different Person,* was nominated for a National Book Critics Circle Award. He died in 1995.

ETHAN MORDDEN spent his youth in Heavensvill, Pennsylvania, Venice, Italy, and on suburban Long Island. He is the author of numerous books on music, theater, and film. His fiction includes the novels *One Last Waltz, How Long Has This Been Going On,* and the cycle of short stories known as the *Buddies* trilogy. He won the National Magazine Award for fiction in 1989.

FRANK O'HARA wrote several books of poetry before his early death in 1966 at the age of forty. His books include *A City Winter, and Other Poems* and *Meditations in an Emergency.* His posthumous books, *Collected Poems (1972)* and *Selected Poems (1974),* were published by Knopf.

JOE ORTON, author of such plays as *Loot, Entertaining Mr. Sloane,* and *What the Butler Saw,* achieved considerable acclaim and notoriety in the mid-sixties. His life and burgeoning career were brought to an abrupt end when he was murdered by his lover in 1967. He was thirty-four years old.

DALE PECK's work has appeared in *Out, QW, The Nation, VLS* and in the literary anthology *Men on Men 4.* His most recent novel is *Law of Enclosures.* He divides his time between New York and London.

ROBERT PETERS has authored over forty collections of poems and criticism, including *Poems, Selected & New* and *Where the Bee Sucks: Workers, Drones and Queens of Contemporary American Poetry.* Seattle's Fantagraphics is publishing a series of Peters's X-rated comic books on the sex life of J. Edgar Hoover.

FELICE PICANO is the author of seven novels, including *The Lure*, *The Mesmerist*, and *To the Seventh Power*; two memoirs, *Ambidextrous* and *Men Who Loved Me*; and a collection of short stories, *Slashed to Ribbons in Defense of Love*. He currently lives in Los Angeles.

JOE PINTAURO, in addition to being a playwright, has written a number of award-winning books of poetry, including *To Believe in God* and *The Rainbow Box*, as well as two novels, *Cold Hands* and *State of Grace*. His plays include *Raft of Medusa*, *Men's Lives*, *Snow Orchids*, and *Cacciatore*.

DAVID PLANTE is the author of the Francoeur Novels, a series comprised of three novels: *The Family*, *The Country*, and *The Woods*. His other titles include *The Catholic*, *The Accident*, and *Annunciation*. A frequent contributor to the *New Yorker*, he lives in London.

RALPH POMEROY is a poet and prose writer with a number of books to his credit. He is also an artist who has exhibited both in this country and abroad. His poems have appeared in such publications as *The New Yorker*, *Poetry*, and *Paris Review*. He is a former associate editor of *Art News* and contributing editor of *Arts* and *Art & Artists* (London). He lives in San Francisco.

PAUL REIDINGER is the author of the novels *Good Boys*, *The Best Man*, and *Intimate Evil*. He grew up in Wisconsin and went to school at Stanford and the University of Wisconsin at Madison. His work has appeared in *SF Weekly*, the *Chicago Tribune*, and the *Los Angeles Daily Journal*, among other publications. He lives in San Francisco.

ROBERT RODI is the author of *Closet Case* and *What They Did to Princess Paragon*. His latest novel is *Drag Queen*. He lives in Chicago.

PAUL RUDNICK has written two novels, *Social Disease* and *I'll Take It*, and the screenplays for *Addams Family Values* and *Jeffrey*. For the play *Jeffrey* he received the Obie Award, the Outer Critics Circle Award, and the John Gassner Award for Outstanding New American Play. His other plays include *Poor Little Lambs*, *Raving*, and *Cosmetic Surgery*.

DAVID SEDARIS, playwright, essayist, radio commentator, made his debut on NPR's *Morning Edition* with "SantaLand Diaries," a recounting of his experience as one of Santa's elves at Macy's. He lives in New York.

BRIAN SLOAN has had stories published in a number of magazines including *NYQ, New Ink,* and *Christopher Street.* He also works as an independent filmmaker. His twenty-seven-minute film *Pool Days* was included in a 1994 anthology of three short films that was nationally released as *Boys Life.* He currently resides in Greenwich Village.

ANDREW SOLOMON, a contributing writer for the *New York Times Magazine,* is the author of *The Ivory Tower: Soviet Artists in a Time of Glastnost.* He lives in New York and London.

LYTTON STRACHEY was a highly regarded historian, biographer, and social critic in the early part of this century. He is the author of *Eminent Victorians* and *Eminent Edwardians.* He died in 1932.

EVELYN WAUGH wrote some of the most savagely witty novels of the twentieth century, including *Vile Bodies, The Loved One,* and *A Handful of Dust.* The television adaptation of *Brideshead Revisited* was one of the most popular shows ever produced in Great Britain. He died in 1966.

EDMUND WHITE has written several novels, including *A Boy's Own Story* and *The Beautiful Room Is Empty.* His books of essays include *States of Desire: Travels in Gay America* and *The Burning Library.* In 1994, he was awarded the National Book Critics Circle Award and the Lambda Literary Award for *Genet: A Biography.* He currently lives in Paris.

TENNESSEE WILLIAMS was one of the most highly acclaimed American playwrights of this century. His plays include the Pulitzer Prize–winning *A Streetcar Named Desire, The Glass Menagerie,* and *Cat on a Hot Tin Roof.* He also published two collections of poetry, *In the Winter of Cities* and *Androgyne, Mon Amour.*

T.R. WITOMSKI's work has appeared in several journals and in the anthologies *Shadows of Love, Gay Life,* and *Hot Living.*

ACKNOWLEDGMENTS

GRATEFUL ACKNOWLEDGMENT
IS MADE FOR PERMISSION TO REPRINT
THE FOLLOWING:

From *Surprising Myself* by Christopher Bram. Copyright © 1987 by Christopher Bram. Reprinted by permission of Donadio & Ashworth. From the novella *I Am Thinking of a Number* by Liam Brosnahan. Copyright © 1992 by Liam Brosnahan. Reprinted by permission of the author. From *The Weekend* by Peter Cameron. Copyright © 1994 by Peter Cameron. Reprinted by permission of Farrar, Straus & Giroux. From *The Mysteries of Pittsburgh* by Michael Chabon. Copyright © 1988 by Michael Chabon. Reprinted by permission of William Morrow & Company, Inc. From *Such Times* by Christopher Coe. Copyright © 1993 by Christopher Coe. Reprinted by permission of Harcourt Brace & Company. From *A Home at the End of the World* by Michael Cunningham. Copyright © 1990 by Michael Cunningham. Reprinted by permission of Farrar, Straus & Giroux. From "Fearless" by Jameson Currier, first published in *Men on Men 5: Best New Gay Fiction*. Copyright © 1994 by Jameson Currier. Reprinted by permission of the author. "Two Bartenders, a Butcher and Me," by Daniel Curzon. Copyright © 1981 by Daniel Curzon. Reprinted by permission of the author. From "Breaking Up with Roger," in *Spontaneous Combustion* by David B. Feinberg. Copyright © 1989 by David B. Feinberg. Reprinted by permission of Viking Penguin, a division of Penguin Books USA, Inc. "Giant Pacific Octopus" from *Counting Myself Lucky* by Edward Field. Copyright © 1992 by Edward Field. Reprinted by permission of Black Sparrow Press. From *The Liar* by Stephen Fry. Copyright © 1991 by Stephen Fry. Reprinted by permission of Soho Press (U.S. only) and David Higham Associates (Canada only). From *Life Drawing* by Michael Grumley. Copyright © 1991 by The Estate of Michael Grumley. Reprinted by permission of Grove/Atlantic, Inc. From *Invisible Life* by E. Lynn Harris. Copyright © 1991, 1994 by Clyde Taylor. Reprinted by permission of Doubleday, a division of Bantam Doubleday Dell Publishing Group, Inc. From "Cruise Control" by John Edward Harris, first published in *Waves: An Anthology of New Gay Fiction*. Copyright © 1994 by John Edward Harris. Reprinted by permission of the author. From "Baseball in July" by Patrick Hoctel. Copyright © 1988 by Patrick D. Hoctel. Reprinted by permission of the author. "Fast-Food Sex" by Andrew Holleran, first published in *Christopher Street Magazine*. Copyright © 1979, 1996 by Andrew Holleran. Reprinted by permission of the

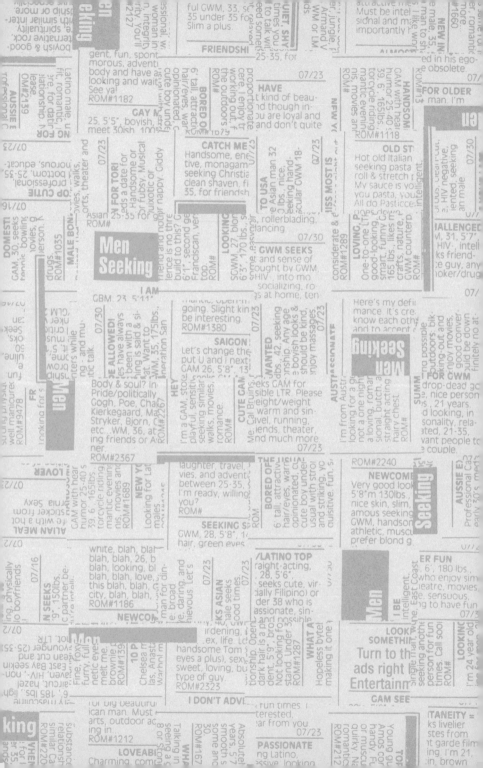